AUDACIOUS

GABRIELLE PRENDERGAST

ORCA BOOK PUBLISHERS

Library and Archives Canada Cataloguing in Publication

Prendergast, Gabrielle, author
Audacious / Gabrielle Prendergast.

Issued in print and electronic formats.
ISBN 978-1-4598-0530-9 (bound).--
ISBN 978-1-4598-0265-0 (pdf).--ISBN 978-1-4598-0266-7 (epub)

I. Title.
PS8631.R448A83 2013   jc813'.6   C2013-902108-6
C2013-902109-4

First published in the United States, 2013
Library of Congress Control Number: 2013936062

Summary: Raphaelle's involvement with a Muslim boy is only slightly less controversial
than her contribution to a student art show.

*Orca Book Publishers is dedicated to preserving the environment and
has printed this book on Forest Stewardship Council® certified paper.*

Orca Book Publishers gratefully acknowledges the support for its publishing programs
provided by the following agencies: the Government of Canada through the Canada Book
Fund and the Canada Council for the Arts, and the Province of British Columbia
through the BC Arts Council and the Book Publishing Tax Credit.

Cover design by Teresa Bubela
Cover artwork by Janice Kun
Author photo by Leonard Layton

ORCA BOOK PUBLISHERS
PO Box 5626, Stn. B
Victoria, BC Canada
V8R 6S4

ORCA BOOK PUBLISHERS
PO Box 468
Custer, WA USA
98240-0468

www.orcabook.com
Printed and bound in Canada.

16 15 14 13 • 4 3 2 1

For Alice

chapter one

Sirens

PARTING

I guess
This is the part where I
Gather with all my girlfriends
To say goodbye.
The problem is that final scene
Transpired already
I'm not sure when or where.
They walked away, one by one
Looked back with a self-important glare,
Or maybe didn't look back at all.

We don't slump across my bed,
Wet red eyes and dramatic voices.
I can't believe you're moving. It's so unfair.
I think I'll just DIE!
Then paint each other's toenails
Pink and blue with glitter
And blow on them until they dry.
Instead I fold jeans and hoodies
And a pink vintage dress I wore
Just
Once.

I throw away much more.
Garish 1960s skirts and shirts
At the last moment I snatch out the pink dress too.
I won't wear it
Again.
It wafts into the charity pile, angel like,
For a girl from the East Side, I think.
I throw in the golden shoes too, and hope they fit her
Whoever she is.

Goodbye, I say to her imagined loveliness.
She waves back from her rain-sagging porch.

Goodbye.

THE LIST

Jill and Casey
So long ago I barely remember.
I left them in the sunshine
Under a papaya tree
Holding hands and crying
As the taxi backed down the driveway.
My heart closed like an envelope
In my bony chest.
Later, when I looked down from the plane
A long white cloud stretched across the horizon.

Megan
Of the lilting words
The church that wasn't Catholic,
And was therefore scandalous.
We rang the bells
And then something unknown
Happened to her father's job.
They went back to Wales.

Claire, brilliant Claire
We wrote songs about Ancient Egypt,
And cut our own hair.
Her parents divorced
And she got the one in Florida.

Jan, who I never called Janelle
She wanted a boyfriend

And when she got one
Had no time for me.

And the rest
Those girls in junior high
Who only pretended
To like me.

I don't care.
I let them go, like the vintage pink dress.
At the new school
I'll start again.

SIRENS: PART ONE

I will leave behind
The paralyzing nightmares
The smell of whiskey

The callous concrete
The sound of a locking door
My insolvent heart

So easily led
Seduced by their Siren smiles
Their swift promises.

Things not remembered
Entirely accurately
Not quite understood

The things I'd rather
Not memorialize in
A journey eastward

I discard, reject
Purge from my mind and soul so
My reinvention

Can begin.

chapter two

DINOSAURS

THE TRIP: PART ONE
OR HOW I LEARNED TO
APPRECIATE VLAD THE IMPALER

If I told of it in rhyme
I could make it seem sublime
The truth, however, was more like
Being skewered on a spike
Or a twelve-hour drive in a hot car with two teenage
Girls, arguing parents and a radio that doesn't work.

THE HOTEL

Read this
Someone wrote on the Gideon Bible.
It will change your life.
That may be, I write in reply,
And mine is a life
That needs changing,
But I don't have the time.

Moments later, I take it out again and sign my name
Raphaelle
A Bible autographed by an angel
Has got to be worth something.

DINOSAURS

These are the reasons we couldn't make the trip in June:
Michaela's baseball
Michaela's grade-eight graduation trip
Michaela's friend asked her to stay for a week
On the island.
Michaela wanted to go to Bible camp
Michaela had to do math at summer school
She's not stupid, Mom says,
Just not much good with numbers.
She's quite good with telephone numbers, I say.
Michaela wanted to go to the end-of–summer-school party
Michaela wanted to throw an end-of-summer-school party
Michaela had to repeat the summer-school exam
The more I think about it
The more inclined I am to categorically declare
This is all Michaela's fault.

By the way, this was an ocean once
Writhing with fish and trilobites.
Dinosaurs splooshed around in marshy lagoons
And ate palm fronds
Or each other.
Now it's dust and sand, dry and hot.
The dinosaurs left this place 65 million years ago
And never came back
I can't say I blame them.

THE TRIP: PART TWO

Beyond the dinosaurs there is nothing to see.
Dad's jokes about cruise control
Make Mom's lips pinch.
I can see her in the rearview
Staring forward, squinting in the golden light.

But as the land flattens out, I am suddenly free.
A giant dome of blue sky above us, my soul
Expands to fill up every empty open inch
No mountains or trees or oil rigs,
The land feels new
Clean, uncluttered.
Like a shaved head,
Shiny and bright.

What are you grinning about? Michaela groans
I feel like we've landed on the moon.
I can tell Mom agrees
But Dad's fingers tap the steering wheel
He grins too, sunglasses on, and begins to whistle

Delighting, I alone understand, in all the unknowns.
What's that plant, he says that afternoon
The purple flower makes Michaela sneeze
And retreat to the car, whining
While we finish our meal.
I savor that purple flower,
And its name I know:
Prairie thistle.

NEW HOUSE

Okay, first let me say: It's huge.
Michaela and I try to count the rooms,
But lose track at twelve.
Our old bungalow eight blocks from the beach,
The one with the blackberry winding up the porch,
The cracked path,
The tiny tiled second bath that no one wanted to use?
It could fit in the three-car garage.
Heated garage, my father says, ominously.

There's a suite—not like our old suite,
Low-ceilinged cave
With dewy walls and unknown smells—
A real suite, bright high windows and its own patio.
Mortgage free, Dad says, *no more tenants.*
Mom pretends not to be pleased.
The girls will fight, she says.

But Michaela is already moving in
Picturing slumber parties, pink-pajama frolics
Late nights of gossiping
Can I have my own phone?
And boys, eventually, one day
Silently, stealthily,
Sliding the screen door closed
And stealing,
Slick and satisfied,
Into the night.

I don't mind. I've picked my room.
A gabled loft above the attached garage.
The "bonus room."
It has its own narrow staircase,
With a door at the bottom.
We could put a bathroom up here
Dad says about a giant closet.
Yes, please, I say.
Even Mom laughs.

There's a window, facing east.
I can see the freeway and the prairie beyond.
The horizon, my long-lost newfound friend.
I make a vow.
At least once a month
I will watch the sun rise.

CORN: PART ONE

The next day, a guy arrives
Tools jangling
And tears apart the giant closet
Business is slow, he tells my father
Which is why he could come today.

Michaela takes a bus to a paint store
By the end of the day the suite is as pink
As the inside of a watermelon
And a trellis of golden vines
Is winding across the walls

At noon, our furniture arrives.
My bed won't fit up the narrow stairs
Within seconds, Michaela has claimed it.
A hammock, maybe, Dad suggests.
Mom phones a futon store.

Dad and I set out
Like consumer Argonauts
The empty car expectant
We will stop for groceries on the way back.

The futon store is over the train tracks,
Past the exhibition ground, the football stadium
And rows of drooping houses
Sweating in the heat.

Dad pulls over and buys corn
From a flatbed truck in someone's yard.
My brother's farm, the tanned kid says, pocketing coins.
A skinny pregnant girl stares at me from the front door.
She's my age or younger.
Her black hair wisps across her face
In a light summer breeze.

The futon fits in the car,
Folded like an origami crane.
The groceries pile on top
They are un-exotic and, Dad says,
Expensive.
I think of the pregnant girl
The tanned kid
And his brother
And hope they eat some corn.

TWO MORE DAYS

Two more days until school, huh Rah Rah?
Dad's nickname for me sounds, as always, like a cheer.
Sis-boom-bah! Rah rah rah!
A better name for Michaela in my opinion.
Still, he calls her Me Me
Which also seems to fit.

Two more days.
I nod silently
And history hangs between us.
New schools, full of promise.
A bloody nose
An empty bottle
A locked steel door
A letter sent home in a sealed envelope
Which I tore open
Right in front of that self-righteous blowhard.
The look on his face still makes me smile.

Raphaelle
Is not adjusting well
We think some therapy would be swell
Or maybe drugs those often work
For those whose teacher is a jerk
Without treatment she may go berserk.

The letter didn't rhyme.
That part I made up.

NEW SHOES

Michaela's feet have grown.
To keep the peace, I get new shoes too.
We trundle to the mall
Dad wanders around looking for the pay-parking
meter
Heat dazed
Until he realizes parking is free.

We deposit him in the coffee shop,
Like a child to day care
Michaela and I take our fifty dollars each
She bolsters hers with pocket money
And birthday money
And buys fat white and silver sneakers
The logo gleams fit to blind me.

I take mine to Walmart
And buy canvas ballet flats
Two pairs:
Red-and-gold-striped and blue and green polka dots.
I plan to wear one of each.
With my leftover money, I get my nails painted black.

Only when we get home
Does Mom remember
We'll need snow boots.

PUBLIC TRANSIT

I will get my driver's license one day
But not today.
Today I practice getting to school.

We have made a decision, my parents and I
Michaela will go to the Catholic Girls School
Wear the knee-length blue pinafore
The gray cardigan
She will be, apparently,
Allowed to wear the blinding-white shoes.
The school is walking distance from the house.

I will go elsewhere.
The Catholic system and I agree to disagree.
And a school full of girls, frankly
Fills me with dread.
I'm going to the public school.
It has an *alternative approach*,
The brochure says, mysteriously.

The bus stop is outside Starbucks.
Caffeine soaked and foam flecked
I board the number 12
Whitmore, the bus reads.
With more what, I think
Dyslexically.
Then lament for ten minutes
That the bus isn't called Whitman.

It rumbles past a park, a mall, a church, a parking lot.
The plan is for me to stay on the bus
Let it complete the loop
The scenic tour of town, and get off again at
Starbucks.
But instead I ring the bell when the school is in sight.
Disembarking in the heat, I feel a slip of fear
Alone on an unknown street.

JOHN CRETCHLY COLLEGIATE
HIGH SCHOOL

It screams
BUILT IN 1962!
Low, bland, utilitarian.
Like a cheap frying pan.
The flag waves listlessly on a rusty pole.

I still have Walt Whitman on my mind.

I make a pact with you
John Cretchly (whoever you are), I say
I have screwed around long enough.
I come to you a reformed girl, in mismatched shoes
Who has a softhearted father and a resolute mother.
I'm perplexed enough to try again
I don't know what you did
To deserve a school named after you.
But now that you are words carved into stone
I will try to learn from you.

ANOTHER LIST

St. Margaret's Preschool
I wanted to play with the boys
They wanted to see my underwear
Who was I to disappoint them?

St. Pius X Primary
Jackie Wengerwich stole my raincoat
So I put worms in her sandwich
And only told her after she had eaten it.

St. Patrick's Elementary
Katie LaBelle laughed about my bloody nose in gym
I opened her locker and let the blood drip
All over her best skating dress.

St. John the Baptist Junior High
I argued in class about the Resurrection
Jeanette Cheung called me a "lezbo"
So I pushed her into a urinal.

I wore a floaty hot pink vintage dress
To a black and white ball
All the other girls were in little black numbers
I glowed in the dark.

And something happened, something foul-smelling
That I can't quite recall.

Someone found me crying somewhere.
There was alcohol involved.

St Francis of Assisi High School
I drew Christ on the cross
Naked and well endowed
I wrote *Jesus Loves Gays* on the blackboard.

I put a macro into the library computers
Every time someone typed *cu*
(As in *cu l8tr*) while chatting
It would add a well-placed *nt*.

It's not like
That word
Was unfamiliar
To me.

SUNDAY MORNING: PART ONE

Dawn comes at 6:30
And wakes me.
The ink of night fades into pink lemonade
A line of orange slices the horizon

The sun peeks up slowly
Rays bisect the dusty sky
Long thin strips of cloud, like stretched-out ribbons
Illuminated by fire
Drift away, their night-time condensation dissipated
By the heat of morning,
By the rising sun,
By the new day.

SUNDAY MORNING: PART TWO

It is time to go to church.
I'm still wearing boxer shorts and an undershirt.
Hardly Sunday Best.
Mom yells up the narrow staircase
Get dressed!
I'm not coming, I reply.

I hear the tension ooze silently up the stairs
Followed by Michaela.
She resents being the conduit between Mom and me
But sucks it up.

Tell her I'm unconfessed, I say.
Who'd sin with you, is Michaela's tart retort.
But she oozes away
And moments later
The front door slams.

I lie in sultry silence
And try out my voice against the slanted ceiling.

I'm not sure if You're listening, I say
But I don't think You can help me anymore.

And in that moment, I shed that biblical autograph
That angelic designation
And am reborn
As Ella.

chapter three

MANDALAS

RAH RAH

This was me:
The one who said the wrong thing
Who crossed the wrong person

Who had the wrong hair
The wrong body
The totally wrong clothes
The wrong attitude

The

Wrong

Color

Dress

The WRONG friends.

I was born in the wrong decade
In the wrong country
To the wrong family

I couldn't do anything right
Except draw
(The wrong pictures)
Which I do
With the wrong hand.

Ella will be different.

ART

I decorate those slanted walls.
Not for me, glossy, fat-haired singers
With inviting smiles.

In a cardboard tube, tucked in amongst our furniture
My life in art has traversed half a continent
And thus deserves an audience
Even if it is only me.

I unroll the painted sheafs.

"An abstract geometry of gouache
After Mondrian"
I flatten it under books.

A pencil seal cub, poking its sleek head up
I couldn't quite capture the curiosity in the eyes.
I roll it backward and pin it up.

A charcoal sketch
The life model, a treat for one class only
Wore a modest bathing suit.
I sketched her nude, regardless
Small round nipples
Like coins balanced on pert breasts
A tuft of hair, arrow of promise.
Mrs. Kott tucked the sketch into a stiff envelope
With a smile
And asked me to take it home.

A watercolor
Bland, floral
There was a sub that day
And I couldn't be bothered.

An acrylic on paper
A bearded man looking in through a window
His eyes were silent lies is scribbled on the back.
And a grade: A+
It's vaguely unsettling to remember
I painted this one in Religion, not Art.
I don't remember
Making Him look so insipid
Impotent
After all
He is OUTSIDE the window.
I pin Him across from the nude
So He'll have something to look at.

YET ANOTHER LIST

These are my school supplies, which I lay on the futon:

Six pencils, sharpened to lethal points
Six pens—three black, three red
I don't care for blue ink.

One large binder
Five dividers
One ream of loose-leaf, divided into five

A geometry set
A ruler
A calculator

All things suggested by a list from the school
For grade elevens, it says
To these I add my own suggestions
For grade elevens:

Chewing gum and mints
Because bad breath is a conversation killer

Tampons, just in case
And anyway, a loaned tampon
(As if you'd want it back)
Is good for a week of superficial kindness
From all but the haughtiest girls.

Chocolate, because sometimes if I feel like crying
Chocolate stops me
Like an inhaler
Stops an asthma attack.

I would like to take an asthma inhaler
Because kids are always losing theirs
And surely saving someone's life
Is worth even more than a tampon.
But inhalers are by prescription only
And Michaela needs her spare.

Lip gloss,
Which is actually Michaela's recommendation.
Dry lips make you feel nervous, even if you're not.
She's thinking of dry mouth
But I take the lip gloss anyway.
It tastes like grapes.
Maybe if I get hungry
I can eat it.

CLOTHES AND HAIR

Michaela tried eight ways of doing her hair
Asking my opinion of every one.
I'm just grateful she has a uniform.

What are you going to wear, she says.
Clothes, I say, maybe underwear.
Don't show them to the boys, she says.
Maybe I'll wear them on my head, I say,
To save the boys the trouble of asking.

She knows about my plan
For mismatched shoes.
I think she secretly approves.
But I'm having doubts.
Mismatched shoes
Are more of a Raphaelle thing.
Ella just wants to blend in.

I tell Michaela about my new name.
She's delighted
And scandalized
And wants one of her own.

Ayla?
Ella and Ayla? I don't think so.
Mickey?
Sounds like a baseball player.
I AM a baseball player.

Okay then.
Kayli?
Too cutesy.
I'm cute.
I fall silent.
She's right.
Kayli is perfect.

THE PLAN

No scenes
No pranks
No vengeful practical jokes
No culture jamming
No hacking
Nothing inappropriate.

I will seek out a middling girl
One not too pretty
But not too weird
And befriend her.

Avoid the popular clique
Too much temptation
And risk.

Join an uncontroversial club
Chess maybe
Or Scrabble

NOT debating
And dear God
Not Bible study.

(But secretly I long for the chance
To do it all again
To see the looks on the faces
As cherished ideas are deflated

Faith is lost
Morals are challenged
I long to curse, and paint nudity
And reveal lies and weakness
And stupidity.
I long to draw the eyes of others
To themselves
And their failings
And away from me
And mine.)

FIRST DAY OF SCHOOL

No one

Looks   at   me

Or   talks   to   me

All   day.

At Starbucks

A   boy   with   deep brown eyes

Who might   have   been   in   my   art   class

Serves me chai.

HOW IT REALLY IS

Kayli brings home two giggling girls.
Their pleats swish down the stairs
To the watermelon palace.
Squeals of delight resonate upward.
Kaaaayyyliiii! I love love LOVE it.
It's SO AWESOME!!
They only emerge to phone their homes
Seven o'clock? No way! Ten!
Okay eight-thirty then, whatever.
No I'll walk.
Jeez the sun will still be up! Chillax!
And slide a frozen pizza into the oven.

Mom and Dad and I
Eat chicken.

HOW I DREAM IT

The Starbucks boy has been saving up his pay.
I leave the mudroom door open.
He climbs the narrow stairs
And in the moonlight, he sketches me,
Nude of course.

We make love
(That part is hard to imagine)
It's his first time too.
He has a tattoo and a pierced navel.
And calls me *Mi Bella*
Because the brown eyes mean he's Italian I suppose.

We take his money
And steal away
East into the night
East until we reach the sea.
We embrace on the sand
Salt water swirling around our feet.

Then I become a mermaid
And swim away.

DREAD

Dawn sears through my eyeballs
At a godless hour
And makes me think
Here on the Plains
With no trees or mountains
To filter the sun
Maybe all the hours are godless.

One school day done
288
Or so
To go
Until I graduate.

288 days to find
A niche, a hidey-hole
A slot to fit into like a coin.
288 days to avoid the kind of crisis
That always seems to find me.

Dad bolts out of the house
Briefcase swinging
Grinning.

Kayli swishes off
With a girl from two streets over
Giggling.

Mom sips coffee
And unpacks another box
Sighing.

I walk to the bus stop
Eyes down, determined
But dreading.

TUESDAY

Lacks the promise of Monday
The resignation of Wednesday
The despair of Thursday
The full strength stop-me-before-I-gouge-out-my-
    own-eyeballs-with-a-blunt-piece-of-chalk
Of Friday.

Tuesday is the day he says:
I saw you at Starbucks, right?

MANDALAS: PART ONE

Ms. Sagal, who teaches art—
Miz, she emphasizes if we slip
And say Missus
I am already privy to the gossip
That she's a single mother by choice—
Gives us squares of blank paper and pencils
And instructs us to draw.

The page must be filled, she says.
We scratch away.
I sneak a look through my bangs.
Puffy Blond is drawing a sunset
Freckle Arms is drawing a flower
Buzzcut is drawing a cross section
Of the *Enterprise*
Not the Starship, understand,
The aircraft carrier.

I carve my paper in quarter sections
Then line by line
Dot by dot
A mandala blossoms
Like frost on glass
And fills my page.

An hour passes.
Sign your drawings, Ms. Sagal says,
And pin them on the board.

Although he sits well away from my desk
Starbucks boy has drawn a mandala too.
And signed his name:
Sam.

TENURE

Dad was a high-school history teacher
And ran a camp for nerds in the summer
Night-owl nibbling at his PhD.

Now he is a professor
Full Professor with tenure
Whatever that means except
I'm pretty sure it means a lot more money.

He used to work school hours
But over The Bridge
So he'd trail in
Slug-tired
Traffic-addled
About an hour after Kayli and me.

Now he works strange hours
Night classes
Meetings
And grading in his den
At midnight.
He has a club
For Byzantium enthusiasts
That meets on weekends

And four graduate students
Who call almost every day

Tenure: from the Latin tenere, *"to hold"*

They certainly seem to have a hold on him.

LATCHKEY KIDS

We were latchkey kids, my sister and I
We walked from the school along the beach
Then eight blocks up. She'd want to try
To turn the lock, but I had to, since she couldn't reach.

Mom loved books, you see, and wasn't happy
Baking treats or mopping floors or growing roses
And nor were we, with her always feeling crappy
Nothing more exciting in her life than snotty noses.

She bought a suit on sale and some shoes
And ventured out in search of inspiration
Because a woman is allowed to choose
Exactly where she wishes to apply her dedication.

The public library was the beneficiary of her gifts
And we two girls soon learned survival skills.
Housewifery's like that, I hear, some it uplifts
The rest, like my poor mom, it nearly kills.

All this has a point. In this new city:
The library has no jobs, Mom says at dinner
My dad looks up, and says, *Oh? That's a pity.*
And this is when my mom starts getting thinner.

DERIVATIONS

Freckle Arms and Puffy Blond don't like me.
This has been made clear in several ways:

They snigger when I come into French class
They nudge each other in the hallway when I go by
They sneer at me in the lunchroom
A silent warning:
Don't sit here
As if I would even try.

I'm wary of them
Their glossy lips hide sharp fangs
And I have been bitten
One too many times.

Freckle Arms and Puffy Blond
Think they're popular
I recognize the desperation
The careful measuring of every word and move
The calculation
Can I afford to slip today?
Where am I on the populometer?

They recognize me too
A liability with my mismatched shoes.
Which I wore BY ACCIDENT
Believe it or not.

Me, they know, they can't afford
At all.

What's Ella short for? Elephant?
It's a cowardly attack.
We're alone in the art room
Apart from Sam.

Shut up, Eugenia, he says.
Not all names are short for something.
Freckle Arms, who signed her flower "Genie"
Glares at him
But shuts up.
They scuttle to their seats
Like scorpions.

Sam leans forward.
What IS Ella short for? he asks.
I hesitate
                    ...Raphaelle
The strange name floats above my desk
Like an unfamiliar scent
A wisp of frankincense.

Sam nods. *Biblical,* he says,
The way some kids might say "radical."
You can talk "Samuel."
As soon as the words leave my mouth
I try to gasp them back.

Sam smiles and sits back.
Actually, it's Samir, he says.

Oh,
I say.
Oh.

SAMIR

It's a Muslim name—NOT Italian.
I looked it up.
I'm ashamed to say
I never met a Muslim before today.

Catholic School is my excuse.
We had some Chinese kids
Who didn't pray
And once a Jew, but she moved away.

MANDALAS: PART TWO

Ms. Sagal talks about our mandalas
She asks us why we chose
To draw something abstract.

I'm feeling bold.
I like them, I say,
The process is meditative
It feels primal.

Someone get me a dictionary, Freckle Arms whispers.
I try to smile congenially
I mean, what have I got to lose?
But Ms. Sagal nods.
Excellent insight, she says.

I turn to Sam
Expecting him to share my pride
But he's frowning
And when Ms. Sagal asks him
He only shrugs.

MIZ

She sometimes brings her daughter
Who sits in her wheelchair
In the back of the art room
Drawing wild swirls
With her spindly
Unpredictable arm.

How old are you?
I say to her after class.
She's fourteen
Ms. Sagal says.

She doesn't speak.
Cerebral palsy.
But she's very smart
She goes to a private school
They're closed today.

Marika is her name.
She smiles at me
A bit lopsided
But beautiful.

THE SHOWDOWN

She actually started to say it:
As long as you're living in this house, young la—
But she couldn't finish.
She laughed
And so did I.

It's something we do as a family
It's boring.
It's important to your father
No it isn't.
What would your Nana say?
She's dead.
Don't you have anyone you want to pray for?

This one stops me.
I could pray for Puffy Blond and Freckle Arms
To stop being so vapid.
I could pray for Kayli
That her asthma would get better
Or her feet would stop growing.
I could pray that someone
Would sit with me at lunch.

I could pray for Samir.
Aren't we supposed to pray
For the conversion of the infidels?

Or is that how he
Is supposed to pray for me?

REGURGITATION

Mom

       threw

           up

               after

                    Sunday

                         brunch

It's not worth mentioning except

                      She

                snuck

           upstairs

       to

    do

it

And I don't think she's really sick.

chapter four

PORTRAITS

HOT CHOCOLATE

It comes over me on the bus
A fug, a mizzle of discontent.

Puffy and Freckle called me fat today.
Not directly
That would be gauche.
They said I looked like an old TV star
Who is famous for being fat.
They said it in front of everyone.

It festers all afternoon
And on the bus it overwhelms me.
Fat.
Useless.
Ugly.
Boring.
Stupid.

Gullible.

Ella short for elephant.
My eyes sting.

At Starbucks, I ring the bell
Stumble off.
Through the glass I can see Samir
The last person I want to see me this way
But my feet seem to feel differently.
They take me to him, smiling behind the counter.
He takes in my expression.
Are you okay?
Hot chocolate, I say.
And bless him,
He seems to understand.
Double chocolate, extra whip?
I ask him how he knows.
Everyone has bad days, he says.

OXYGEN TENT

Kayli starts wheezing at dinner.
Mom walks away from her full plate
And prepares the nebulizer.

Kayli crawls onto the couch
Curls up, looking small.
Play tent with me, she says.

We used to do this with a lacy crocheted blanket
Thrown over our heads.
She would wheeze behind the mask
With me concocting tragedies.

Two Dickensian sisters wasting with consumption
A mother and daughter poisoned by toxic gas
(From where was never clear)
Gasping through their last minutes
Or our favorite imagining
Siamese twins
One hale and healthy, one near death,
An arrow in her breast.
Oh the sorrow, the desolation, the wretchedness.

The crocheted blanket cannot be found.
I improvise a plain white sheet.
The effect is dramatic
Without the lacy holes,
We can't see the outside world

And no one can see in.
So instead of tragedies
We share secrets.
I cheated on a math test,
She whispers through the mask.
A boy in French offered to sell me pot, I counter.
I think my history teacher is a lesbian, she says.
And then coughs until Mom lifts the sheet
Gazing pucker-browed as the coughs subside
Then lets the sheet waft back into place.
Mom looks thin again, Kayli says
Although this is no secret.

VEILED WOMAN

She yells at him outside Starbucks.
I linger
Out of sight.
I'm not really spying.
I just don't want him to see me
And be embarrassed
Or something.

She yells in a throaty language.
I wish I could understand
What she's saying.
I'm not really spying
I just want to know what is going on
And maybe help him
Or something.

She yells in front of everyone
And when she turns and strides away
I see her face.
I'm not really spying
I just want to know who she is
And what she means
To him.

An olive-skinned glaring moon
Surrounded by a carefully fixed black veil
She climbs into the back of a black car.

She's young and pretty.
I'm not really crying
I just have dust in my eye
Or something.

FORBIDDEN

I saw you watching me, he says.
I only nod.
Are you religious?
Catholic, I tell my coffee cup.
He asks me what I'm not allowed to do.
I begin to enumerate the Commandments:
Steal, covet, bear false witness…
He interrupts.
What are Catholics especially not allowed to do?
Mostly sex stuff, I say
Then blush and blush.
He chuckles.
No, you know, playingwithyourself
Hmmm.
No birth control.
Really? None?
No abortion.
Of course.
No execution.
How often does one have the opportunity…?
Catholics don't condone execution
By anyone,
For any reason,
Ever.
Oh. Homosexuality?
Obviously not.
What about food?
No rules really, not anymore.

We eat fish on Friday but it's not compulsory.

Alcohol? Gambling?

Yes, please, we're Irish.

He chuckles again.

He has a nice chuckle.

What about you? I say

What aren't you allowed to do?

Don't get me started, he says.

I stir my coffee.

Pork, alcohol, carnivorous animals.

What? No tiger burgers?

No. No insects or reptiles.

Yuck.

No dogs.

Who would eat a dog?

No OWNING dogs. They are unclean.

Really? What about cats?

Cats are fine. To own, not to eat.

Phew.

No mind-altering drugs.

That's a pity.

Pretty much all the same sex stuff.

I thought as much.

But contraception is okay in marriage I think.

Oh? That's much more sensible.

No usury.

What's that?

No idea. Something to do with lending money.

I never have any so it wouldn't matter.

No drawing pictures of people or animals.

What! Why?

It's like trying to create life.

Like playing God?

He shrugs.

Is that why you drew the mandala?

Why did YOU draw one?

I remind him primly that I explained it in class.

He looks like he doesn't believe me.

Anything else? I say.

No gambling.

His eyes fall, black lashes like prison bars

That's why my sister was yelling, he says.

She found a lottery ticket I bought.

All I hear at first is "sister."

Eventually I can speak again.

Did you win?

No.

Why did you buy the ticket if it's forbidden?

He looks up through the prison bars.

I need money. I want to buy a dog, he says

And chuckles.

SNOWFLAKES

Falling so softly,
like thieves in the frozen night.
They steal the city.

FOUR-WHEEL DRIVE: PART ONE

Dad drives us to school
Because somewhere in the mental chaos
Of unemployment
Mom forgot all about snow boots.

The Range Rover plows through drifts
Like desert sand
Like jungle scrub
Like rugged mountain streams
Just like in the ads.
But they never use snow in the ads
It's far too suburban.

Dad gives random academic advice
Kind of a demented morning pep talk
To Kayli:
Just think of fractions like half-price sales.
Mention the Bolsheviks. That makes them crazy.
No, it's kingdom, then phylum, THEN class…
Because Bilbo is an atypical hero who doesn't want…
She escapes into the snow
A Siberian refugee
Into the arms of St. Mary.

While we plow on to the public school
He's more subdued.
Any classes you like?
Art.

Any teachers?
Ms. Sagal.
Any teachers you don't like?
Librarian's a total despot.
Is there such a thing as a partial despot?
I snort, with what I hope is derision.

The unasked question, which remains unasked—
Any friends, Raphaelle?
—is also left unanswered.

WATERCOLORS

Halfway through art I sneak a glance
Samir is looking back at me.

Without speaking he lifts up his page
And shows me a watercolor coffee cup
Overflowing with whip
And chocolate

I say nothing
I just lift up my page
And show him
A watercolor dog.

RENT-A-GEEK

Puffy and Freckle have an entourage
frnds 4evr
Each member has a role.

The homework helper:
A plain girl in expensive clothes.

The project:
A pretty girl in shabby clothes
I want to throw a hardback copy of *Emma* at her head.

The drug supplier:
A sk8r dude
Pretty sure he's got nothing stronger than pot
Maybe coke.

The narcissistant:
Who helps them feel beautiful
u r so hot. no u r!
She's pretty but not as pretty as them.

The chauffeur:
A chubby, effeminate guy
With an incongruously masculine car
Bought for him no doubt
By a father who is worried his son is gay.

I realize today
A spot might have opened up
4 me.

The rent-a-geek:
Who fixes their pink laptops
When they won't play MP3s.
Or download reality TV.

Their old rent-a-geek got a bespectacled college boyfriend
They met at a comic shop (really!)
And she has no time anymore
For Puffy and Freckle.

They watch me with my MacBook
And helping Ms. Sagal load the PowerPoint
The one about Leonardo Da Vinci.

OMFG!
I can't help laughing actually
If they offer me the "role"
And I take it
About all the fun I could have
Messing with their hard drives.
I wonder whether they will
Or I will.

IT'S FUN TO BE FORBIDDEN

I'm not a Muslim
I have pierced ears
I ate bacon for breakfast
I drew a smiley face on my hand
I pluck my eyebrows
I sing and dance—not always in private
I drank one of Dad's beers last night
My wrists are showing
Even my name is forbidden
(*Some think it blasphemous*
To give a child an angel's name
Especially a woman, Samir says, tightly)
And I'm sitting in a coffee shop
With an unrelated boy.

GOOD WORKS

Mom has been volunteering
At a place called Marion House
A homeless shelter.
I see the worry in her eyes
When the snow swirls in the yard at night
It's so cold, she says, *I hope they have enough beds.*

She bakes
And sneaks Dad's older sweaters into boxes
With socks bought on sale, in bulk
At the Army & Navy store.

She tells me about an old woman
Who calls herself The Phantom
Who has only one eye
Who gets ejected from the rec room
For swearing

It's the Lord's work
She says at dinner, not eating
Just stirring potatoes round and round
Jesus Himself would have loved these women
And made them disciples.

I try not to laugh
As a comic book opens in my mind
Jesus Christ and the One-Eyed Phantom.

The movie version
Will be rated R
For Coarse Language.

FACES

In art we do portraits
In pairs
I sketch Puffy Blond
And make her look fatter than she is
She sketches me
Badly
Froglike
Maybe you really look like a frog, she counters
Freckle Arms sketches Samir
Like a WANTED poster
Intense stare
Emotionless
Even though he was laughing the whole time
About my drawing of Puffy Blond

Ms. Sagal starts to say
It's okay
Sam
if

But he snatches up the pencil and paper
And someone appears on the page
Not freckled
But beautiful.
Soft and expressive

With a light in the eyes
That I recognize
As me.

CHANGES

We weren't always like this
My family
We were "moderate"
My sister was at fashion school

Then it happened

I know what he means
The planes
The TV
The war

My mother was chased from a drugstore
My father lost customers

He owns a landscaping company
And a fleet of snow plows
I have seen his trucks.

My sister married a conservative man
And took up the veil
And gave up school
And turned her eye on me
She changed my clothes
And my mind changed with them

I have heard the teasing,
The whispers about the long-sleeved shirts

And long pants
Even in gym.

Every cruel word makes me feel closer to her
To my culture
My history
My people
My God.

So now you are conservative too?

His fist rests on the table
Millimeters from mine.
Unclenching
He raises one finger
And closes the circuit between us.

I don't know what I am

Electricity flows
Fingertip to fingertip

I
    know
        how
           he
               feels.

DETAILS

I try to memorize him
In that moment
His black hair
Close-cropped and wavy
His dark eyes
Like pools of strong coffee
The faint shadow
On his upper lip.

His lips
My God, his lips
The way they press together
Tense and troubled.

His hands
With a little ink stain
On the second finger
On the left
(He's left-handed too!)

His clothes
Long-sleeved shirt, buttoned all the way up
Sensible jeans
That don't hang off his ass
(I HATE that)

I carry him home with me
When we part
Awkwardly
His memory is a work of art
That only I can see.

THE TOOTHBRUSH I FOUND IN MOM'S PURSE

Toxic
Odorous
Oh my God
Tedium
Has
Become
Regurgitation
Undoing
Shaming
Her

Totally gross, I know
Only that's how we found out last time
One toothbrush
Tucked into the lining of
Her purse in a plastic
Bag. The smell was unmistakable
Right then Dad confronted her
Uprooting her
Secrets and lies
How do I do the same?

chapter five

MARTYRS

THE VIRUS

Freckle got a nasty virus
Not that kind
Although I wouldn't be surprised.

My antivirus expired
I don't know how to fix it
I suck at things like that

All this delivered with a sweet smile
A tilted head
Like she never called me "elephant."

It won't boot up properly
Everything is super unstable
I can't even Skype

I accept the proffered pink laptop
And set about examining
The inner workings.

I'm SOOO grateful for this
I'd just DIE without "Pinky"
Can you fix her?

I think so, I say cautiously,
Taking care to look her in the eye when I ask for
Her passwords.

She surrenders them innocently
Then she and Puffy, giggling,
Scribble their phone numbers on my homework.

TWO SONNETS FOR STINK-EYE THE LIBRARIAN

I

I use my spare to point and click and search
To cleanse the pink computer of disease
Poor "Pinky" cannot function so besmirched
She's like a cat that wriggles, rife with fleas.
It's difficult but still I have a plan
To winkle out the bug that caused the crash.
At once I sense some disapproval and
Glance up, as I delete poor Pinky's cache.
The despot stares behind a magazine
Her condemnation of all things plugged in
Apparent in her glare at my machine
Because to her what's not a book is sin.
Above the sick and epileptic screen
I see Samir who smiles and mouths *She's mean.*

Yet unperturbed I note private details
Of friends and boys and other juicy news
Dear Freckle Arms won't know that her emails
Will reappear on an account I choose.
I'm quite the spy, I snicker to myself
Though I resist the sabotage today.
Stink-Eye still lurks in wait behind a shelf
To pounce on any kind of disarray.
Then she appears behind Samir and screams
Get out! Get out! We don't allow that here!
Apparently well used to harsh regimes
Samir says *Bitch!* and storms out with a sneer.
Old Stink-Eye, paralyzed, emits a gasp
Stone-faced, like she was bitten by an asp.

EXTREMISM

She moves again
And retreats to her office
Excited murmurs follow her.
Her slamming door
An exclamation mark
Then silence.

I lean over the table
And turn Samir's screen to face me.
I can't read the Arabic letters
But I get the gist.

A row of black-and-white photographs
Young men
Each with the bottomless eyes
Of those
Who are already dead.

My heart blisters in my chest
My head floats away
My Samir?

GABRIEL'S BIRTHDAY

He lived for three minutes
Gurgling out his first and last breaths
In her arms too early
There was some dreadful complication
That took her womb too.

Every year this day
She carries around a tiny knitted hat
Tucked into her pocket
Like a handkerchief.

We tiptoe around her
And grieve for
Our lost angel

Imagining
That sibling

We'll never have.

HUNGER: PART ONE

I find Samir at last
In the back corner of the lunchroom
Sitting with a dark-skinned boy I don't know
Not eating
Both reading.

He sees me and smiles
And invites me to sit
Did you forget your lunch?
I say, and offer him half my sandwich
(I check that it's not ham first, that much I know)
It's cheese, I say.

I'm not hungry.

(Those words give me a chill
Mom eats nothing at breakfast
At dinner
At all.)

I chew discreetly.
What are you reading? I say.

He shows me the small book
More Arabic letters.
The Qur'an.

That's like the Bible, right?
Your holy book?

Is it good?
(Oh my god what a stupid question!)

His friend looks up and grins.
It's very good, he says, with an accent that Samir lacks
You should read it.
It will change your life.

I'm still trying to get through my own holy book, I say

(Though this is a lie.
I gave up ages ago
And anyway, there's only so much
Change a girl can take.)

Actually, Samir says
I'm not that good at reading Arabic.

Me neither, I say
And we all three laugh so loud
That people turn to look at us.

Chuckling
(I love his chuckle)
Samir returns to his pages.

I eat, and through the corner of my eye
Watch Samir
Not eating.

HISTORY

Samir's friend heads off to the library
Ma'a salama, he says to us as he leaves
Khalid is from Somalia, Samir explains
And tucks his little book away.

Where are you from? I ask
(Why haven't I asked before?)
Palestine, he says
Searching my eyes for a moment

Do you think of it as Israel?
I'm not sure what I mean to say but
"I try not to think of it at all"
Is what comes out.

Samir nods
Good answer, he says, then searches again
Those eyes, behind the prison-bar lashes,
Unravel me.

You don't have to tell me more, I say
(I watch the news)
But I get the feeling anyway
That he's about to change the subject.

He leans forward
You're beautiful, he says

And takes a moment to enjoy my reaction
Before leaving me

To knit myself back together.

THE MIRROR

The girls' room on the bottom floor
Smells bad
Of cigarettes and worse
Broken rules
Sometimes broken hearts
I once found Freckle crying in here.

But in a school full of crowds and open plans
It's private enough.

I gaze in the spit-flecked mirror
Trying to see
What he sees
In me.

GOOGLE

Tells me it's Ramadan
Wherein Muslims don't eat or drink
During daylight hours at least

Kind of like Lent
But not.

Lucky it's nearly winter here
Daylight hours are short
I can't help worrying though
About the Muslims in Tasmania
Or Argentina

It seems unfair
But when it comes to faith
What doesn't?

FACEBOOK: PART ONE

Finally I can no longer resist
I log into Freckle's Facebook
Just for a minute.

UR back. LA fxd Pinky? Yay!
Writes Puffy Blond
Reducing me to two letters.
LA, like the smog-drowned megalopolis
I can relate I suppose
To the smog.

Then later: *Is LA w Sam now?* Freckle writes.
Jealous? writes Puffy.
To which Freckle responds
with a series of barficons.
:-o~
:-O=
%O<
And that sort of thing.

It's a bit disappointing.
I expected something scandalous
Or libelous
Or at the very least
Useful.

FACEBOOK: PART TWO

And I guess
Since I'm disguised
As someone else
I feel brave

For a reckless moment
I look up a name
And another name
From the past

And another
And another
Until they are lined up
Like crime suspects.

Feigning innocence
Behind their racoon eyes
Claiming they never
Locked that door

Their cool beauty
Their witty comments
So close and immediate
It's easy to forget

I unfriended them
In the dark

In the cold
Because they only

Pretended.

AFTER ART

Ms. Sagal asks me and Samir to stay
We linger by the door
His arms are crossed
Tightly
As though he's afraid
His heart might jump out of his chest
Like I am.

Are you all right Ella?
Ms. Sagal says to me
You look flushed.

God God God
I want to die.
Samir pretends to cough.

The winter art show is coming up
She tells us
Taking care not to say "Christmas art show"
She needs another piece from each of us
To fill up some empty walls
I'm asking all my best students to help out.

Samir says something about time
Can you use your spare?
He says he can
And so do I

The art room is empty in that period
So you can work here.

Alone
With Samir.

AFTERMATH

Then she just, like, leaves!
She even closes the door.
Samir uncrosses his arms.
Well, he says, *this is awkward.*

Then we both laugh until we have to sit down.
I like how you laugh all the time.
You mean even though I'm miserable?
Are you miserable?
Isn't everyone?

Not me, *not right now,* he says
And asks me to help him stretch a canvas.

I want to do a huge acrylic
Something eye-popping
Like Lichtenstein or Warhol.
What are you going to do?

Something controversial, I say
(Without really knowing why).
I like to agitate, I add.

It's working, says Samir, *I'm pretty agitated.*

RULES

I'm not really allowed to have a girlfriend
I mean my parents would not approve
I know you probably think that's dumb
But it means a lot to me.

I really like you though
I meant what I said in the lunchroom
I probably shouldn't have said it
You're right, I am miserable

Do you know what it feels like
To be pulled in two different directions
When neither of them feel completely right?
I'm coming apart. Fragmenting. Like cubism.

Please don't cry.

ABOUT THAT WEBSITE

And then I ask him:
What were you looking at
That day in the library?

The staple gun punctuates the silence
Bang!
He has beautiful eyes
Bang!
He has cara-melt-in-your-mouth skin
Bang!
All just out of reach.

I fold my hands in my lap
Kneeling there on the floor
The giant canvas we've made
An altar
To something
Unfinished.

My cousin, he whispers
He was one of them
They call him
Martyr
But to me
He was just
My cousin.

HIS LIES

No one notices
When I disappear
After dinner.

No one can hear me
Sobbing
Above the garage.

No mother to rock me
She's lying down
With a "stomachache"

No father's pep talk
"Plenty more fish in the sea" etc.
He's grading papers

No sister to conspire with
Or plot revenge
She's giggling on the phone in her room

No one here
But me
And his silent lies.

Palestinian
Muslim
Conservative

To me
He is just
Samir.

SIXTEEN

And never been kissed
Not on purpose anyway
A drunk boy once engulfed me
At a party

In a narrow dark passage between
Beer and vomit
He pressed me against a lurid orange wall
Tongue and hands exploring
Like a surgeon
Looking for lumps.

You're not Rebecca, he slurred
Eventually
Like I didn't know

I watched him stumble and
Pinball down the hall
Thinking

Poor Rebecca.

MIDNIGHT: PART ONE

I miss my old friends
Kayli says
Then cries in my arms
Like a little girl

I'm so worried about Mom
She sobs
And seconds later she's wheezing.
The inhaler appears
Hisses medicinally
And disappears
In practiced motion.

I hate it here
This house is so big
I feel like I'm a million miles away
From you
From everything
Dad's never home
The weather sucks
The girls at school are dumb
Superficial pointless Barbie dolls
My classes are way hard
I'll never understand algebra

Finally she looks at me
Seeing my red eyes
My snotty nose

What's going on with you?

FOUR THINGS I NEVER SAY TO MY SISTER

One:

Every time I look at your perfect body
Dancer's legs
Pitcher's arm
Every time I look at how perfectly
Perfect
You are
I want to disappear.

Two:

Once when Mom was sick
She got so angry at me
(And at you
But you had already run off)
That she screamed at me
I would trade both you girls
For Gabriel!

Three:

There's a dark black hole in the past
Somewhere in junior high.
A cold place where nothing can escape
Don't fall in

And if you do fall in, look for me
Because that something dark and cold
Won't let me go.

Four:

At my worst moments
I blame you for your cloud
Of giggling friends and confidence
Because I was trying to be you
Observing and emulating so intently
I lost my footing in the fog
And nearly died for it.

WHAT I DO SAY

Is it about the thing?
Kayli says
The "thing" I don't quite
Want to remember or discuss.

It's about a boy, I say
A boy? Really?
Don't act so surprised
Sorry. What's his name?
Samir
What kind of name is that?
It's a Muslim name
You rebel! How exotic
Nothing has happened
So why are you crying?
Because nothing has happened
So make it happen
It's not that easy
Sure it is. Men are all alike
Not Samir.

(I don't bother wondering
How my fourteen-year-old sister
Knows so much about men.)

He likes me
But he can't have a girlfriend.
So he just wants to…

No! Nothing like that.
It's his religion or something.

Religion, Kayli says with a sniff.
It screws everything up.
Especially sex.

chapter six

ANGELS

SPARE

We prep canvases
Painting gesso in silence.

Samir sighs
And sits back on his heels
(He's painting on the floor)
Like Jackson Pollock, he says.

Are you going to dribble snot all over it? I ask
He laughs explosively
And knocks over his water.
We rush around with paper towels.

I'm kidding, I say, I love Pollock.
So audacious.

Audacious, he says
That should be your middle name.
Then he sighs again and shakes his head
That was so corny.

I want to touch him
Suddenly
So suddenly
That he won't be able to stop me.

DREAMING

I dream

The tanned kid and pregnant girl
With the corn
Standing in the yard
The snow drifting down on them

Marika
Her awkward body transformed
Elegant
Flying with streams of color

Samir
Outside my window
Like a Montague

I wake to a car alarm.

The house sleeps yet restlessly
Somewhere, someone paces
I'm not sure how I know.

My mother
In the kitchen
Walking back and forth
Between the stainless steel,
Box of Shreddies tucked under her arm
Swallowing handfuls
Crying.

I duck out of sight.
She would not want me to witness this
Nor do I
But it's too late.

WHAT COMES NEXT?

I know Dad knows.
He hears the retching
Sees the red knuckles
Smells the breath
Feels Mom's ribs when they hug
He must know.

Is it that he's busy
With his new job?
Is it that Kayli and I
Are too busy
With our new schools?

Why hasn't somebody
Said
Or done
Something?

BLACK

The first thing Samir does is paint the canvas
Black
Three layers of black
It has to be pure
Like night
Sunless
I'm beginning from nothing.

He lets each layer dry
For a day
Waiting.

There are comments
When art class begins
Are you painting the contents of your brain?
Says Freckle.
Samir leans forward and whispers to me
Her heart.

Pardon me, I say.
He whispers again
Her heart
His lips a centimeter from my ear.
Pardon me, I say again
Until he gets the game

And whispers
Your hair smells nice.

For the rest of the class
I can't draw a straight line.

NINE SMALL CANVASES

A word swims around my head
Audacious
In my mind it forms a picture
A line of women
Saying *screw you* to convention
Of any sort
Saying *shove it* to the expectations
Of society
Of school
Of close-minded fools
Saying
This is who I am:

Arab

Unemployed

Disabled

Asthmatic

C
Stops me.
I'll get to that later.

Indigenous

Old

Ugly

Single

I want to include bulimic
But there is no *B* in *audacious*.

THE PROCESS

So I start with photographs
Mom, in her robe, with coffee and newspaper
Unemployed

Kayli, in the nebulizer mask
And pajamas
She woke up wheezing
Asthmatic

I ask Ms. Sagal
She loves the concept
And poses
Proud to be single

Her daughter poses too
Lopsided smile
Disabled

I ask Mom if I
Can come with her to the shelter.
The Phantom
It turns out
Loves to pose for pictures

With her gnarled face
Gaping hole where her eye used to be
She is ugly
Yet

Now I begin to understand
What *audacious* means.

Because behind that ugliness
Is beauty, as old and deep as the ocean.

CORN: PART TWO

After school, I take the bus
Across the tracks
Hoping I will remember the house.

There it is
Still sagging
Now under the weight of
Wet snow.

The truck, half submerged in the driveway
Empty and abandoned-looking.

It's an awkward moment
When she comes to the door
A tiny baby asleep on her shoulder
But she invites me in.

I'm sixteen, she says when I ask
My name is Nina, and yes, I'm an Indian
I didn't use that word
I said "indigenous."

I tell her the name of my school
Nina laughs
I went there. We would be in the same grade
Except for...
She pats her sleeping baby with a smile.

When she hears of my project for Ms. Sagal
She poses willingly
I was good in art, she says
And lets me hold her son
While she braids her hair.

DEATH AND TEARS

Ms. Sagal checks my progress
(Samir paints in the corner,
His canvas turned away from us.
It's a secret, he says.)

Do you think I can include
A photograph
Of someone who is dead?

I clarify: taken when they were alive of course!

(Here she smiles with relief I can see.
I wonder what does she think of me
I mean I would have to be sick in the head
To include a photo of someone actually dead.)

Who? she says, recovering her poise.

My grandmother
She was old
Eighty
When she died two years ago
Exactly five years after Gabriel...

Suddenly without warning
I'm crying.
Ms. Sagal steers me to a seat
I tell her everything

Poor little Gabriel
Mom's grief
The vomiting.

Then Samir appears beside me
With a clean white handkerchief.

NOMENCLATURE: PART ONE

Nana loved angels
She stitched them into quilts
And named my mother Angela.

Mom
Dreamed of at least three kids
Named for the archangels
Raphael
Michael

And of course
Gabriel

But only got
Two-thirds of the way
There.

The weight of that name
Is sometimes a mountain
With a cave of secrets

And sometimes a feather
Floating on a puff of air.

chapter seven

JUXTAPOSITION

OLD

Nana
Wouldn't have
Liked it maybe
Being called
Old
It's like
A prize that
Nobody thinks they want
And when they have it
They pretend they don't
Until they die.
Not me
I
Long to
Get "old" because
Being young
Sucks.

NOMENCLATURE: PART TWO

So that leaves me with "Arab"
Which despite everything
I have to look up.
And it doesn't help:
> Arab (ăr'əb) n.
>> 1. A member of a Semitic people inhabiting
>> Arabia, whose language and Islamic religion
>> spread widely throughout the Middle East and
>> northern Africa from the seventh century.
>> 2. A member of an Arabic-speaking people.
>> 3. An Arabian horse.
>> 4. Offensive Slang. A waif.

(That last one makes me think WTF?)

Samir tells me
Yes, we are Arabs
Sometimes people call us
"Israeli Arabs"
Like Palestine is just a myth
Or a half-remembered dream.
So you prefer to be called Palestinian? I ask.

Samir thinks for a long time
He gets that smoky brooding look in his eyes
The one that dissects my heart
Lays it out on the table
Like a pithed frog.

We would be called anything, he says
To have our country.
I let that swirl around us, like mist
Then dissipate
Before I ask:

Would your sister pose for me?

Samir whips out a phone
Speed-dials
And speaks in Arabic.

(God, I love the way the
vowels make his lips move.)

He hangs up
And without irony says
She will ask her husband.

HALA: PART ONE

She's beautiful close up
Gorgeous in fact
Although of course I can't see her hair
Or the shape of her body

But her eyes are like Samir's
Deep chocolate pools
Sadness
And pride.

I like the way you dress, she says
Eyeing my loose men's Levi's
Dyed purple (by me in the kitchen sink)
And flowered blouse over a long-sleeved T-shirt.

Modest
Not like most…
I feel myself redden
And to cover it snap her picture.

I was going to say
A very rude word
I'm sorry.
I snap and click in silence.

Do you know why I quit fashion school?
She asks suddenly.
I shrug
Because your husband…?

It was before I met him.
We had an assignment
To design and make a line for little girls
Who would model in the show

She shakes her head
Her black scarf twists
She removes a pin
And secures it carefully.

I designed pretty dresses
And jeans with flowers on the knees
The girls were nine and ten.
Children.

I know what she is going to say
I myself have marveled
At the state of Kayli's attire (or lack thereof)
On more than one occasion.

The others, my classmates
Made these girls
These children
Look like prostitutes.

Tight hot pants
Crop tops
Knee boots
And dangling earrings

Made them walk
Swing their hips
Wink and sashay like whores
Her eyes mist over

Then she strikes a pose
Hidden but for her resolute face
And looks more like a woman
Than anyone I have ever seen.

HALA: PART TWO

Has Samir told you my secret?
She says.
I shake my head
I have only told close family so far
But I trust you.

She cups her hands
around the embroidered cloth
Of her tunic
Cradling the curve of cotton
That's not quite there yet.

I snap a photo.

Four months, she says
With a coy smile.

RAVENOUS

I meet Samir at a falafel place
On Cornwall.

I'm starving, he says, shoveling tabouli
Ramadan was brutal
I haven't stopped growing yet
I'm hungry all the time.

Then he's embarrassed
And eats in silence.

Will your sister tell your parents
About me?
What's to tell?
He must see
The hurt in my eyes

No, I didn't mean it like that
She thinks we're classmates
That's all.

No, you're right, I say
What's to tell?

Then I leave him
To eat alone.

WHITMORE

And on the bus home
I cry
Like some stupid girl
Who got her heart broken
By a desert mirage.

I ride around the loop
In the dark
Back to the falafel place
But he's gone.

At home I search the mirror
For the one he said was beautiful
She's there
But where am I?

I who makes enemies
Like some people make coffee
I who scorns fashion
And popularity
And the cachet of
Having a boyfriend
Whom teachers fear
And principals dread.
Where is Raphaelle?

Folded up in Ella's pocket
It doesn't matter
In a few days
Everything will change.

IN THE ROOM ABOVE THE GARAGE

No one must
      C
Me take this photograph

This is for
      U
Samir

For
      U
Freckle and Puffy

For
      U
Mom and Dad and Kayli

Because I'm done
PreteNding

I strip
And stand
Legs slightly open
Facing the camera
On a timer
I can't help smiling
Though my face won't show.

FLASH!

Then I dress
And go downstairs
To make a cup of
    T

DIGITAL PHOTOGRAPHY

Last week I installed a lock
On the door at the bottom
Of the narrow staircase
Because getting caught
Taking pictures of your own...

You know...

Would be majorly embarrassing
Never mind
With my history
Would probably result
In a trip to the shrink.

Mom and Dad have scoped one out
In this new city
For sure
Just in case.

So private and secure
I print and crop
And glue to the canvas
The last picture
The **C**
For
Me.

STRATEGIES FOR THE DISPLAY OF ART

Let's go for an eclectic approach
Ms. Sagal says
And I agree
I hate when they group things
Or try to make some kind of flowing theme
Or narrative
Or chronological journey
Like they are telling you
How and what to think.

Instead we try for symmetry or asymmetry
Clashing colors, conflicting ideas, Ms. Sagal says
Juxtaposition.

Buzzcut,
Who is hanging his military cross-sections
Between a bouquet of flowers
And an abstract decoupage in soft yellows,
Clearly agrees.

I love that word, he says to me
Unexpectedly.
Juxta-position
Is that like "missionary position"?

I can't help it.
I burst into laughter
Which echoes through the hall.

Buzzcut laughs with me
And soon we're hanging freshman art together
Commenting scathingly
And hilariously
Where necessary.
But he is genuine
And appreciates what deserves it.

EIGHT PANELS

It's amazing
Says Ms. Sagal
So lyrical and moving
Don't you think so?
She says to Buzzcut
Who lingers nearby

It's awesome, he says

I have hung eight
Of the nine canvases
In a bright prominent space
Between a large lavender-toned watercolor by Puffy
And a blood-soaked comic
By the former rent-a-geek
About a terrible dystopian
Snowboarding school

My centerpiece
The **C**
Is drying, hidden away, at home.

Still Ms. Sagal gushes
It's really excellent work Ella
I'm so proud to be your teacher
And one of the subjects
Marika will be delighted.

She admires the calligraphy
Disabled
I feel a small pang of guilt
Tomorrow, when Marika comes to the show
No one will be looking at her picture
Or any of the other eight canvases

When my **C**
Is hung **Up**
No more will I be
T-cher's pet.

GROWTH SPURT

I'm starving, says Buzzcut
Who signs his drawings—
Which are actually excellent—
David.

The next thing I know
We are on the way
To the falafel place.

He orders two extra-spicy chicken rolls
While I have some baklava
And crazy strong coffee.
Why do boys eat so much? I ask.

Growing, he says, mouth full
I'm already six-one
But my brother is six-four
So you never know.

I think of Samir
Suffering through Ramadan
When as if by magic
He appears.

With his sister, and I guess her husband
A handsome man with glasses
Hello Ella, Hala says
We do some introductions.

Her husband is Yusif
Samir knows David from calculus and art
They grunt a weak begrudging greeting
I'm Ella, who took the photos.

I emailed the shots to Hala
They're wonderful, her husband says
I'm looking forward to the show.
(Oh dear, think I.)

They sit on the other side
Out of earshot.
Weirdos, David says.
Get that nun suit they've got her in.

He chews thoughtfully
Still, I'd like to see what she looks like underneath
But that's true of all girls.
I smirk with false reproach.

Tomorrow
For me at least
He will get
His wish.

MY PROCESS, FOR ANYONE WHO IS INTERESTED

I started with the photos
Which I printed on plain paper
In black and white
The contrast slightly enhanced
Bold and graphic

Then I pasted them to canvases
Which had been pre-painted
In various shades
Feminine and fresh
Minty green or raspberry pink

Some portraits I tore or cut
And reassembled
Carefully
Letting the gaps
Just barely show

One I cut up like a jigsaw puzzle
Another in zigzags
Like Charlie Brown's shirt.
I left only one intact
(Guess which one)

After the glue dried
I varnished them

Some with crackle finish
Some antiqued
Some sepia-toned or vaguely metallic

One I varnished in pure clear satin
It will shine like a beacon
Because in the end
It is the one that speaks
The whole truth about us all.

TRUTH

No one is completely disabled
Marika has her arms and her smile
No one is ever old
If they don't feel old
No one is totally single
Or alone
The Phantom is not ugly
Not even a little bit
Kayli might be asthmatic
But that is something she HAS
Not something she is
Mom has no job
But that doesn't mean
She has nothing to do
Even the girl with the baby
Didn't use the word "Indigenous"
No one word can encompass
Ten thousand years of history
And five hundred of heartbreak
Like "Arab"
A language
A people
A religion
A country lost
And fragmented
And cobbled back together
By strangers
One word is not enough.

But we are all
Women
And all
The same
Down there.

ART SHOW HAIKUS

I hang the last part
Surreptitiously, alone
Before we open

My parents approach
And are shocked but smile bravely
Kayli simply laughs

David says, *Jeez-us*
And soon there's a crowd of them
Boys ogling my bits

I drift away, faint
With adrenaline and power
Perusing the art

There's tension in here
Something more than the C-word
Is raising hackles

An edgy crowd mills
Gathers, accuses, argues
Over Samir's piece.

ROOF

Are you mad at me?
I ask Samir
His square shoulders a silhouette
Against the streetlight snow haze
Of the rooftop parking lot

I saw him disappear up here
When things got, well
Tense
In the art show.

It was foolish of me
Arrogant in fact
To think that I was the only one
With a controversial idea.

His giant canvas
Oh God it was so stunning
But apparently
There are parents at our school
Who objected to the implication
Of a Star of David
Reduced to a shadow
Of glossy glaze on matte black
Obscured by a Palestinian flag
Made with collaged news reports
Of Palestinian deaths
Or suicide bombers

And graphic photos
He got from who knows where.

Never mind
There was his beautiful pregnant sister
Next to a picture of my snatch.
Which of course
Caused quite a sensation of its own.

Why would I be mad at you?
He says facing the dark.
Below us
On the front steps of the school
A couple is leaving
…expecting to see that sort of thing…
One of them is saying.
…what they call art these days…
Says the other.

Meanwhile, inside, I know
Ms. Sagal is struggling
With certain parents
And their friends
On one hand
And trying to stop David
From taking cell-phone snaps
Of my open parts
And uploading them
To Facebook.

Samir turns
I thought it was beautiful
Even the center panel?
Someone says
(Not Ella, Raphaelle.)
Samir grins
Especially the center panel.
He chuckles
My sister was shocked
But I think she secretly loved it
She was an artist once too, after all.

RUM

Were you shocked?
I ask him.
Not really, he says,
I expected something outrageous
You didn't disappoint.
And anyway
It's not like I was seeing something
I haven't imagined a million times.

It takes a moment for that to sink in
And in that moment he crosses the distance
Between us
I know you didn't mean it to be
But for me
It was kind of hot.
He's so close
I can smell his breath
Cinnamon and something
Rum?

Are you drunk?
I ask, barely believing
Or breathing.
I'm not a very good Muslim, he says.
Me neither, I say, stupidly
But he laughs
One hand slides into the hair spilling from my hat
The other passes me a bottle from his coat pocket.

The first gulp burns
The second stings
The third I don't even feel.
He downs the last dregs
And lets the bottle fall.
Before it even lands
He's kissing me.

chapter eight

PORNOGRAPHY

KISS

Seconds pass
Or days and nights
His other hand finds my waist
And pulls me, urgently
Close

A small moan escapes
One of us
I'm not sure who
As our tongues mingle

I sneak my arms inside his coat
And circle his chest
Through his sweater I can feel
His heartbeat.

Are you cold?

His breaths come quickly
And hard
As though he just won a race.

Samir, I say,
Samir
And lift my face to his

Raphaelle...
He exhales, like a spell
Into my open mouth
And his lips
Seal it back inside me.

HUNGER: PART TWO

Are your parents still here?
He whispers,
His lips tracing the shape of my ear.
They left, I say
I said I'd take the bus home.
What about yours?

I told them not to come.
He kisses my mouth again
I was hoping I could steal away
With you.

Where will we steal away to?
I ask, when he stops to breathe.

ESCAPE PLAN DELIVERED BREATHLESSLY AND INTERMITTENTLY, BETWEEN KISSES

Somewhere warm, like a beach
With dolphins swimming in the waves
White sand and palm trees
And a salty lagoon
We can float together, holding hands
Naked.

Or a cabin, high on a mountain
With a log fire
And a big soft rug
A kettle,
I'll make you all the hot chocolate
You can drink.

Or a sailboat, far out to sea
We'll have a box of books
And art supplies
We can paint and read
All day
And all night we'll…

Lie together letting the ocean
Rock us to sleep
Like children
Innocent and free, no parents, no school
No religion
No you, no me.

HUNGER: PART THREE

Instead, when it gets too cold
We take a bus to the falafel place
Sitting in the back
Making out.

People stare
But we don't care
At first.

But as we get closer to downtown
Samir pulls away
Mouths a piece of cinnamon gum
And offers me one.
We smell like rum.

I'm confused at this change of tone
But he explains
The people who own the place
Go to our mosque.

I'm not hurt
Yet I feel burning behind my eyes
Which I cover by yawning.

So we order falafels
Which he devours
And I pick at, feeling only
Hunger for him.

JEALOUSY: PART ONE

Why did you bring David here?
I'm expecting this question
And decide honesty is best.
No idea, I say, at first and then

I suppose some part of me
Thought you might be here
I wanted to make you jealous
As if David would ever…

Samir gives me one of those looks
David should be so lucky
Then he shakes his head, with a sad smile
Oh boy, I'm in trouble, he says.

I don't know why
I wanted to make him jealous
I know we're both in trouble now
For more reasons than one.

We could, like he described,
Just run away
Ella might do it. But Raphaelle
Wants to watch to the end.

There will be repercussions
An assembly maybe, about tolerance, about "The Middle East"

Or classes for girls
"Our bodies, our decision" and the C-word.

That sort of thing
And my parents, his parents
Trying to outdo each other
In tempered reproach.

DISAPPROVAL

Because they will pretend to be modern
My parents at least
Cross-cultural relationships are difficult
My mother will say

Meaning a Catholic like me
And a Muslim like him
Can never love without the kind of effort
That we're both willing to give

(As if she would know.
She met Dad in St Brendan's choir.)
Samir's parents will be more forthcoming
You are forbidden to see her. It is a sin.

I am a sin, forbidden
That should bother me
But all I can think of are his words
As he left me at the corner of my block:

I love you.

DAD: PART ONE

We're worried about you.
This is how he always starts.
It's always late
Just me and Dad
And a plate

Of cookies, that's always there too
For our little heart-to-hearts
I usually end up crying
Eventually
Sometimes without even trying.

We thought things would be different here, new
But we're back playing our old roles
He's right, things haven't changed
He and Mom still think
I'm deranged.

We are the same, us four, that's true
A family photograph full of holes
Secrets kept from one another
Hunger, fear, doubt, loneliness
And a missing brother.

Is this something you're working through?
He means my painting, like he guesses
I've been molested or hurt.
I haven't, except by
That word I'm trying to subvert.

Poor Dad, he hasn't got a clue
It's just that I'm addicted to these messes
Always looking for a way
To screw up, fall down, wash out
I've become my own cliché.

CENSORSHIP

Censorship is anathema to artistic expression
Is how Ms. Sagal begins.
Predictably someone says: *what's "anathema" mean?*

A Google war breaks out in the back of the class
Brief and intense
As Freckle and Rent-a-Geek tap on their iPhones.
I can see Ms. Sagal struggling
To not roll her eyes

Anathema, Rent-a-Geek says at last,
A person or thing detested or loathed

Ms. Sagal lets that sink in.

However, she continues, *certain types of images*
Are considered especially powerful
And are thus restricted in some way
Like pornography

That word hits me like a falling bookshelf
Slow at first, then engulfing.

It's not pornographic, says Samir.
There are whistles and catcalls
Which he ignores

There are places in the world
Where a woman's wrist
Is considered indecent
And others where clothes aren't worn at all.
Who's to say what's pornographic?

Ms. Sagal sighs, and closes the door.
Of course you're right, Sam
Some of the most beautiful art in the world
Depicts female nudity
Nevertheless there is a question
Of appropriateness

(God in heaven, I hate that word.)

I just wanted to discuss this in class
So you would all understand
Especially you Ella
Why the center panel has been removed.

There are nods and murmurs
People seem to think this is fair.
But unexpectedly
I begin to seethe

Take the whole thing down then, I say
Because

AUDA-IOUS
Is not a word.

It sounds like "a deus"
Which is Latin for God
And therefore the opposite
Of what I
Mean to
Say.

Ms. Sagal nods, with a hint of a smile
I respect your wishes of course.

REAL ART

Ms. Sagal stops me and Samir
As the class files out
Real art requires risk, she says
And a certain willingness
To be exposed
And vulnerable
Not just to scrutiny but to criticism
And even condemnation.

As Samir and I listen, he reaches for my hand
And squeezes.

Well done, Ms. Sagal says.

PUBLIC DISPLAYS OF AFFECTION

We leave art class still holding hands
She didn't say anything
About taking down my painting
Samir says, pulling me aside
To a row of drab lockers
As students stream by.

Your piece is dangerous, I say
But not obscene.
There will be fallout, discussion
But not censure.
Still, I think you had some people
Agitated.

Good, he says, with a cheeky smile.
Then he leans forward and whispers
I desperately want to kiss you.
So do it, I say.
What do I care who sees
Or what they think?

He looks like he's about to
But suddenly he lets go of my hand
And takes a small step back
Glancing over my shoulder
Cool and detached.
I turn to look.

His friend Khalid approaches, frowning
Salam, he says, *maljadeed?*
Samir shrugs. *Nothing*, he says.
Khalid gives me a frank look
Then turns back to Samir
Expectantly.

I'm not completely stupid
I know what's going on
Khalid disapproves of me
And thinks Samir's affection
Is improper, and no doubt
That I'm a firebrand.

Salam, Khalid, I say
As though I say "Salam" everyday
I was tempted to say "Shalom" instead
But thought better of it.
Khalid smiles coldly
Then speaks to Samir in Arabic.

I'll be there later, Samir says
He exhales as Khalid leaves
I'm sorry, he says, *that was not cool.*
I only nod and cross my arms defiantly
I'm just delaying the inevitable
My parents are going to freak.

And you, Samir, what will you do?
Pretend you don't know me?
Promise never to see me again?
There is only one acceptable answer
And questions like that
Should never be asked.

JEALOUSY: PART TWO

Later, in the library
David finds me.
Are you okay?
Fine, I say, why?
You look, I don't know, agitated.
I laugh at his choice of words.

We sit in silence for a moment
Finally he speaks
I just want to say I'm sorry.
For what? I ask, but looking up
I see something in his eyes
That makes me catch my breath.

He looks, unbelievably, like he's going to cry
Like a child, frightened.
What's wrong?
He doesn't answer
And is still staring at me
When Samir appears beside him

Hey Sam, David says to the tabletop
Samir doesn't answer.
There is hostility, even menace, in his posture
David looks up, perplexed
Can I do something for you, he says
You can go the fuck away, says Samir.

I've never heard Samir use this word before
It's unexpected and violent
Like a gunshot
But David gets up to leave
Chill dude, he says, *we're just talking*
Talk to someone else, Samir says.

LET ME MAKE THIS CRYSTAL CLEAR

I don't belong to you
> Or anyone else
I don't take orders from you
> Or anyone else
I don't appreciate you
> Or anyone else
Interfering in my private conversations.

Is it me who says this
> Or someone else?

TAKEDOWN

I feel like a shirt
That's been washed too many times.
Faded and worn.
I've run my entire love-life cycle
Beginning, middle and end
Wash, rinse and dry
In one 24-hour period.

Thus I'm under the covers
When the doorbell rings.
There's something hard in Dad's voice
When he calls up the stairs.

There's a policeman at the door
But Kayli
And Mom
And Dad are right there.

Samir?

But there's no accident
Not that kind anyway.
Next thing I know
I'm getting my coat.

DAZED

This isn't real

They didn't confiscate my laptop and camera
And drive me away in a police car
Did they?

I'm not sitting here
With Dad beside me
Across from a detective
Am I?

He didn't just say:
Child pornography
Or
Disseminating
Explicit
Material
To a minor
Did he?

He didn't just read me my rights
Did he Dad?
Daddy?
Dadda?

SLEEPLESS NIGHT

A clerk took pity
And locked me in an empty windowless office
Instead of in a cell.

The fluorescent light flickers
I lie on a lumpy sofa, under an itchy blanket
Trying to piece it together

Sometime, around three AM
I remember David's cell phone at the art show
And his apology.

WHAT DAD LEARNED OVERNIGHT

Dad turns up at dawn
With a lawyer
...*sixteen-year-old girl you should be ashamed of yourselves
is this some kind of fascism over a photograph what has this
world come to how dare you keep her here overnight with
the drug dealers and hookers what were you...*
I think I like My Lawyer.

Now this is what I know:

David, who turns sixteen in three days,
Took a cell-phone shot of my artwork
Just the center panel
He sent it to some of his hockey friends
One of whom is only thirteen years old
Bad luck
The thirteen-year-old's father is a Mormon minister
Worse luck
David's father is a public prosecutor
Worst luck
Someone needed to be blamed

And that someone is me.
The one who's been suspended from school
The one who might go to jail
Who might have a record
Who might have to register
As a sex offender

For ten years.

Oh yes.

Raphaelle

Nice to have you back.

chapter nine

BOOKS

MORAL SUPPORT

You've really done it this time
Kayli says

Mom and Dad have both
Carefully articulated their
Measured outrage
And unconditional support
But I know secretly
They were expecting
"Something like this."

But Kayli is genuinely impressed
Splayed across my bed
Yelling through the bathroom door
While I soak away the jail filth.

You got ARRESTED.
That is just so totally epic fail.
Thanks, I say.
I'll NEVER live up to that.
All right, let it go.

I emerge in my pajamas
As disinfected as I can get.
A SEX offender,
I mean total etch-a-sketch huh?

She means, would I like to erase it?
But before I have time to consider this
The doorbell rings again.
Maybe that's the police
Coming for you, I say.

Kayli snorts as she rolls off the bed
And trundles down the narrow staircase
I stand there, in the quiet alone
Stare at the wall
And try not to cry.

Slow footsteps pad up the stairs
I don't even look up

Raphaelle?
In two strides Samir has crossed the floor
And wrapped me in his arms.

A BOY IN MY ROOM

You knew, didn't you?
        Is what I say to Samir
In the library, with David
You knew what he did?

I heard it from Khalid
        He says in a soft voice
It was all I could do not to strangle David
Right there in the library

And I yelled at you, I'm sorry
        I don't even know why I did that
I understand about your parents
My parents aren't going to be thrilled either.

Raphaelle, is someone up there with you?
        Mom yells, as if on cue
Could you ask your friend to come downstairs?
We'd all like to meet him.

She thinks we're up here making out
        Even saying it makes my heart race
Mom, please can I have some privacy?
We're just talking about school and stuff.

You've been suspended, I hear
        Bad news really tweets fast these days

It's not fair; it's David's fault
Ms. Sagal has been suspended indefinitely too

I'll tell them she didn't know about it
       This is true after all
She's a single mother; she needs her job
Maybe they'll go easier on me, since I'm a kid.

SAMIR'S SIDE

My parents are furious
Remember I said that Hala
Secretly loved it?
Well Yusif, her husband,
Was somewhat less enthused.
Khalid goes to a prayer group with him

And told him
About you
And he told
My parents
And...
They were talking

About sending me to the Muslim School
You know the one, out on the prairie?
It's a forty-five-minute drive each way.
They said they'd buy me a car
That's how mad they are.
Hala managed to convince them

That you are just misguided
And need direction
And that we should be charitable
But I should not seek to be alone with you
Or be intimate in any way.
They actually said that

"Don't be intimate in any way"
I'm not sure what ways they have in mind
Although I can certainly think of a few.
It's nice to see you smile
Still, a car would be cool.
Oh, my father wanted me to give you this.

A SMALL BLUE BOOK

Penguin Editions
With Arabic and English
The Holy Koran

Perhaps I'll read it
And mend my rebellious ways
See the light, maybe

It's his father's gift
I'm speechless but understand
He thinks I'll convert

Samir's face shows me
Embarrassment but some hope
Our love will prevail.

See, I'm forbidden
So when Samir looks forward
He sees us apart.

Now is not enough
I suppose I should be touched
Yet I want to laugh.

Me as a Muslim
Is just as funny as me
As a Catholic.

For in that instant
In that flash of clarity
Something starts crumbling.

LOST IN DECEMBER

Are you coming to Mass tonight?
Mom says after Samir leaves.
(His departing kiss still tingles on my lips)
Why? I say
I'm pretty sure it's not Saturday
And anyway I hardly ever
Go to Mass anymore
Mom looks at me
Something in her expression
Exasperation?

It's Christmas Eve, she says.

CHRIST IS BORN

We put on quite the show

The felon
I walk as though shackled
Just for fun
People actually look at my ankles
NO ONE GETS SHACKLED ANYMORE
I want to yell
But I can't
Because it's church.

The skeleton
Mom looks extra thin
In her black church dress
And two days without sleep
Haven't helped her sunken face

The consumptive
Kayli wheezes through the sermon
Sucking on her inhaler
Shaking
Sucking
Shaking

The drunk
Near the end, Dad
Who had a brandy
Before we left
Gets the hiccups.

DEAR SANTA

Please make this a dream
Please make me a different person
One who would not do something
So stupid.

Please make Mom start eating
And stop barfing

Please make Kayli breathe better

Please make Dad stop pretending
Like nothing's the matter

Please Santa
Make me
Believe
In you
Again.

AFRAID OF THE DARK

Sometimes the dark is velvet comfort
Soothing the chaos in my head.

Sometimes the dark is as menacing
And cold as a locked steel door.

Sometimes the dark brings slumber
And escape from the drama of my day.

Sometimes the dark awakens
The things that seek to trap me.

Sometimes the dark relaxes
The nerves that coil around me.

Sometimes the dark paralyzes
The muscles that would rescue me.

Sometimes the dark is as quiet
And familiar as a library on Sunday.

Sometimes the dark rings and echoes
With mocking jealous voices.

Sometimes I ride the dark
Like a deep blue wave to dawn.

Sometimes in the dark
I drown.

MARION HOUSE

For as long as I can remember
Mom has disappeared
On Christmas morning.

After the croissants
And fresh-squeezed juice
And presents of course

She loads up a box and drives off
Leaving Dad to entertain us.
But today I ask to go with her

We cruise through the quiet streets
Deserted but for the odd cat or sparrow
Huddled (not together) by a heat outlet.

Marion House is attached to a church downtown
It's a bland building
That looks a lot like my school

Inside, ghosts and wraiths, invisible ones
Society's rejects line up politely
For Christmas brunch

Turkey, stuffing, cranberry sauce
Potatoes, yams, corn and peas
It's my job to prepare dessert

Christmas cake made by church ladies
With a dollop of whipped cream
Flavored with artificial brandy

After dessert there are presents
A local bookstore has donated books
And socks and hats have been knitted.

THE PHANTOM

I remember you
Camera girl
Come to take my picture again?

She reeks of whiskey
Unbelievably
It's barely 11 AM.

Do you have any red socks?
Red is the color of love you know
It's passionate

The word "passionate"
Is lispy and slurred
Because of missing teeth and liquor.

What's this book about?
Shopaholic? What's that?
Don't you have that vampire one?

I go and check.
But all the books have been given out
And tucked away in bags and shopping carts.

What about something serious?
You know. Literature!
What do they think we are, children?

Without knowing why
It just seems right
I give her the little blue Koran.

What's this? Arabic and English?
Read it, I say.
It will change your life.

THE WORST CHRISTMAS EVER

When we get home
Kayli is wearing the nebulizer mask
While she and Dad
Watch *The Wizard of Oz*

The turkey is glowing gold in the oven
And filling the house with
A sleepy, winter smell
The smell of hibernation

That's what Christmas is, I think
It's some primal memory
Of ice-age winters
When the family settled in

Never leaving the cave
Until the snow melted
Living off fat reserves
And stories in the night

Now reduced to one day per year
Though the fat and the stories
Still figure prominently
In our Christmas sojourn.

We eat copiously but this year
Quietly, because the conversation
Will naturally stray to topics
Best left for other days.

Mom eats and eats and we watch,
Grinning until she goes upstairs
I follow and wait and eventually
Force the door and see.

SIRENS: PART TWO

I have heard the Sirens singing
On Christmas Day
Calling me
Urging
Me
To sail mindlessly into the rocks
To doom my shipmates
To crush my ship
And then give
Myself
To
Their beauty, their promises
Their tantalizing lies
Their false joy
Their song
Is their
Trap
The sirens' truth is so hard to look at
An ambulance is on the way now.
I hold Mom's clammy hand
While Kayli cries
And Dad
Cries
Too

Mom threw up too much and fainted
And hit her head on the way
Down to the floor
Beside the
Toilet.
Where Christmas colors, green, white and red,
Are bile
Clean tile
And blood.

chapter ten

ALONE

And by the time the ambulance arrives Kayli
Is in a full-blown asthma attack so
They bundle her away too with
Dad riding shotgun

Call a cab he says to me
Urgently I call and call and
Call there is no answer I
Try Samir but no one is there either

David lives nearby but of course he
Is out of the question then
I remember a row of loopy letters and
Numbers scrawled on my math homework

Genie says one it rings and rings and my
Ears ring with it but no one's home or they
Don't answer on Christmas Day I try
The other *Sarah* trembling until I hear

Hello Puffy says It's Ella I say I'm
Sorry to interrupt your
Christmas she's not concerned *we're*
Jewish we just ordered Chinese food

I tell her everything hardly
Caring I'm crying hysterically minutes
Later she's at the front
Door with her mother

A round soft woman who
Folds me in her arms and lets
Me cry all over her cashmere before
We rush away.

EMERGENCY ROOM

Mom's going to live
That's all I can remember
About the ER.

CLEANING SUPPLIES

Kayli is discharged
Four hours later.
Puffy's mother,
Who asks me to call her Rachel,
Comes back to drive us home.

Kayli feels much better
They've juiced her up with steroids
So she's wide awake
Flip you for cleanup
Heads you choose, tails you lose.

I get heads, and choose the bathroom
Kayli takes the dinner table gratefully.
Mop and bucket
Gloves and bleach
I survey the damage

Sponging, wiping
Squeezing pink-tinged water
After everything looks like nothing
Happened in here
I sit down on the toilet lid

And reach over and lock the door
I decide I like this little room
It's quiet and there are no windows
I could be anywhere
Or anyone.

KAYLI THROUGH THE BATHROOM DOOR

Are you coming out?
Ever?
Great Christmas huh?
This is totally beyond Britney
What a family.

LOCUM SOCIAL WORKER

How we got through the next day
I'll never know
But on the morning of the twenty-seventh
A social worker shows up.

She's flustered and anxious
And frequently checks the file
Asking Dad to leave the room
And speaks to me alone.

Where is your mother today? she asks
I tell her and she scribbles some notes
How do you feel about that?
I shrug, and don't tell her

I feel terrified
And helpless
And guilty
And angry.

And also, I realize, bewildered.
I ask her why she's come
She glances at her file
Because of the pornographic photo.

It's art, I say, not pornography
I was thinking she was here
Because of Mom
Apparently not.

Why did you take the photograph, Ella?
I barely recognize the failed name
It's Raphaelle, I say
Causing her to check her file

But she hardly misses a beat
Do you want to be someone else?
Yeah, I'd like to be you
You're obviously a great success.

A second goes past
Before I realize I've said this out loud
Finally she clears her throat and says
Do you feel like a failure?

And so our awkward little dance continues.
I think I might fail art, I say
Getting my teacher fired, getting arrested
Not my best work.

Was all that intentional?
No.
You took the photograph by accident?
No.

But it's not a dance is it?
It's a hunt, and I'm the prey
You had some idea of the outcome?
I guess so, not Ms. Sagal getting fired.

But you knew you'd be in trouble
Yes. I suppose.
You knew it was wrong?
No. Weird. Not wrong.

Do people get into trouble for being weird?
I do, obviously.
Why do you want to be weird?
I shrug again and don't say another word.

Although of course I know the answer.

WEIRD

Because if I'm weird
And ostracized and friendless
It's not personal.

FALLOUT

Later the lawyer calls
And says the social worker
Told the prosecutor
That I know right from wrong

Which is news to me
Because I thought
Staying true to your artistic vision
Was right.

But I guess I was wrong.

chapter eleven

SNOWFLAKES

IN CASE ANYONE IS WONDERING

By the way
Mom has checked in
It's a "private clinic"

She's going to stay
Because she's so thin
And very sick.

PHONE CALL

I heard what happened
Did you try to call?
There's no reception at my uncle's
I'm so sorry
I should have been there for you
Are you okay?

His voice is like ambrosia
It fills me up
And before I can stop it
Tears are pouring down my face
It's just so good to hear your voice
I say, trying not to sob.

Me too
I wish I could come over
But
Well
I'm hiding in the downstairs bathroom
Just to make this call.

This is the worst Christmas ever, I say
That's why I don't celebrate it
He says, and I laugh.
That's the sound I love
I'm going to sneak out and see you
I promise.

Come over anytime, I say
I'm never leaving the house again.
I'll leave the mudroom door unlocked
You can come right up to my room.
Then I just listen to him breathe
Before he says: *see you soon.*

REPORT CARDS

In the midst of it all
Two letters arrive
End-of-term report cards.

Mine is ironic
Decent grades
Glowing comments
Especially in Art.

Ella has a real gift in art,
Her technique is excellent
Her vision is confident and meaningful.
Well done.

And yet, here I am, under arrest.

Kayli's on the other hand
The perfect normal daughter
Looks like this:

Math: F
Kayli is not grasping the basic concepts
French: F
Kayli has not completed any assignments
History: F
Kayli rarely hands in work or participates

English: F
It's obvious that Kayli has not done the readings
Biology: F
Kayli has not passed any of the quizzes

Dad studies the reports for a few minutes
Then goes into his den and closes the door.

NEW YEAR'S EVE

Kayli is grounded
And I'm on self-imposed house arrest
But Dad's going to the clinic
To be with Mom.
They're having a little New Year's thing.

Before he goes
We have
"The talk"

I have to say
I'm disappointed
I thought we'd be happy here
New house
New city
A new beginning
But instead we're falling apart
Something has to be done
But I don't know what it is
And I need you girls
To help me figure it out
Because clearly something is not working.

Then he straightens his tie and leaves.
Kayli turns to me and says

He noticed.

MIDNIGHT: PART TWO

Popcorn
And a movie
Kayli falls asleep
On the couch

Boredom
And cheap champagne
I tuck a blanket around her
And go up the narrow stairs to bed

Midnight
And fireworks crackle
In the distance
The mudroom door clicks open

Footsteps
And the stairs creak
I sit up, listening
Samir appears in the shadows

Silence
And snowflakes in his hair
He shrugs off his coat
And lies down next to me

DESIRE

We kiss
And more
His hands are soft and warm
And strong.
Gripping my thighs
Through flannel pajamas.

We still haven't spoken a word
Since he arrived.
But he has taken off his sweater
I caress his bare arms
And slide my hands inside his T-shirt.

His muscular body is unexpected
Dangerously sexy.
And soon
We are both breathless
With desire.

DECISION

I have condoms, he whispers
I note the optimistic plural
And lean back
To look into his eyes
Do you want to?
He asks, twisting a strand of hair
Around his thumb.
Yes. No. Do you?
Yes. No. Yes.
I've never done it before. Have you?
Yes. I mean, no!
Yes or no?
He's smiling
No. I've never done it.
So…
I'm in enough trouble already.
Is it okay if we wait?
No. I mean, yes. Of course.
I've waited sixteen years
I can wait a little longer.
Do you want to stay? Do you want to leave?
Yes. I mean no. What?
We giggle in the dark
Tired and happy
And fall asleep
Like spoons in a drawer.

WAFFLES

This far North, deep in winter
Dawn arrives late
Accompanied by the smell of waffles.

Samir is still curled around my back
Asleep, his breath on my neck
I open my eyes

In the doorway blinking
Stands my father, in a flowered apron
Breakfast, he says.

Samir and I
Appear in the kitchen
Five minutes later.

Bacon? says Dad.
Just a waffle, thanks, says Samir
I don't eat bacon

Dad serves a waffle
Are you vegetarian? he asks
Muslim, sir, says Samir

Dad freezes over the juicer
Good, he finally says. *I hope that means*
You respect my daughter's virtue.

Dad! I say, and Kayli dissolves into giggles
But Samir is earnest
Of course, he says.

VIRTUE

It's an old-fashioned word
That means "asset" or "value"
Like that's all a young woman
Is worth.

Maybe it came to mean
What it means
Because people couldn't bring themselves
To say "vir-gin-i-ty."

Samir is contrite
When he heads out into the cold
I feel bad about bringing condoms
Your father is right.

I can take care of my own virtue, thanks
I say, I don't need my father's help,
Or yours for that matter.
Though it's nice that we agree.

He kisses me
And clomps off to the bus stop
Leaving deep footprints
In the new snow.

BAD-NEWS DAY

I expect a lecture
But instead I get
The four worst words
I have bad news
Dad delivers them gently
But has the sense to preface them with
Mom's okay but

I have bad news
Charlotte Connelly died last night
Who?
I say.
She froze in the park
Drunk I suppose
Who can blame her
It was New Year's Eve after all.

Then I realize
I never knew her name.

The Phantom is dead.
Picture the scene:
The red socks
The gaping eye hole
The smell of whiskey

I can't help smiling
When I think of Father Martinez

Identifying her
And finding
The Koran
Clutched in her cold dead hand.

She got the last laugh
Audacious until the very end.

FINAL REST

Mom cries when we tell her
Dad said that she would
She's with Jesus our Lord now
Mom says, *God is good.*

When I tell Samir about it
He feels basically the same
But he says, *Allāhu Akbar*
Same God, different name.

PARADISE LOST

And yet looking for
The Phantom in paradise
I still see darkness.

The French get it right
They have one word to mean both
Heaven and sky too.

The Phantom's last breath
Rose up in the winter wind
And made the sky home.

chapter twelve

BLACK INK

PLEA BARGAIN

Mom's suit, bought on sale
Almost fits me
But My Lawyer makes me change

You need to look young, she says
Inscrutably, *but not cheap*
Nothing sexy

I settle on the purple Levi's
With a pink T-shirt and gray hoodie.
It has a duck on the pocket

Perfect, My Lawyer says
You look about twelve.
And mentally challenged.

Funny.
That's exactly how I feel.
I put on the mismatched shoes.

The prosecutor
An assistant of David's dad
Has a proposal

A lesser charge
Contributing to the delinquency of a minor
A fine and probation

My Lawyer thinks I should accept.
And if I don't? I ask
You could do time, she says.

And leaves me
To talk to
My dad.

IN MY OWN DEFENSE

No because
I haven't done anything wrong
No because
I am a minor myself
No because
It was David who posted the photo
No because
It's my body to do with what I like
No because
The photo isn't pornographic
No because
Ms. Sagal liked it
No because
Samir liked it
No because
It's the best and most true thing
I've ever done
I'm sorry Dad
But no.

THE REALITY OF SINGLE PARENTHOOD

I look up Ms. Sagal on 411.com
I know she lives near the school
Because she walks to work
She's not hard to find
Even though I didn't know
Her first name is Veronica

2874, Suite 12
Gray apartments by the strip mall
I think for a moment
This must be the wrong place
But then I see the hand-built ramp
Into the ground-floor patio

She's surprised to see me
Behind her, Marika is watching *Nova*
Something about the Hubble telescope
Ms. Sagal invites me in
And pours tea
In mismatched cups.

The lumpy sofa, the vague smell of damp
The books and art things crammed on shelves
And medical-looking machines
Bottles of pills on the counter
It all coalesces into something:
Ms. Sagal can't help me.

Marika's school must cost a fortune
Not to mention her therapy and drugs
And there's no Dad to help out
And Ms. Sagal is just a teacher
Not a plumber, after all
Oh my god, what have I done?

NEGOTIATION

Can you make them
Give Ms. Sagal her job back?
I ask My Lawyer.

It's the school's decision
The court can pressure them of course
But in exchange for what?

JUSTICE
I want to scream
But instead I say

If I accept the plea bargain
And do whatever community service they want
And pay the fine

Will they give her back her job
Because her daughter is disabled
And she needs the money?

I can't guarantee that
Says My Lawyer
They are two separate issues

So I could accept their offer
And Ms. Sagal, who is innocent,
Could still lose everything?

How is that fair?
How is any of this fair?
Says My Lawyer.

PURGING: PART ONE

When I get home
I throw up in my new bathroom
Which is ironic
Because Mom comes back today.

She's put on weight
And looks much better
And hugs us girls
Like she will never let us go.

We follow her
As she moves through the house
Throwing away secrets
And bulimic's accoutrements

Toothbrushes, Ziploc bags
Laxatives and diuretics
Stashes of candy bars
She lets Kayli eat one; I decline.

It's a new start, says Mom
Hauling the load out to the trash
Kayli grins and cheers
But I have heard this before.

Maybe she doesn't remember
The two previous times we did this
Kayli was always running away
But I'm not ready to celebrate yet.

BACK TO SCHOOL

School starts again
I'm not welcome
Which suits me
I sleep in.

Kayli's principal calls
Wants a meeting
Kayli refuses
Stays home

After a very late lunch,
Mom who is already
Well sick of us
Takes charge

Pencils are sharpened
Books are opened
Homeschooling
Starts.

EMPTY SPACE

It says more about you
And what you intended to say
Than even the artwork itself

Everyone knows what should be there
My piece is up in the library
And that insipid watercolor

And in between we left a large
Empty space
People have been writing on the wall

"Free speech" and "No censorship"
"My body—my decision"
I saw the girl who wrote that

She didn't think anyone was looking
Some have drawn pictures:
Boobs and butts and…

Signed them—"By Asthmatic"
"By Ugly" "By Disabled"
Stink Eye wants to wash it off

But can't because
There's an informal "honor guard"
All day.

Kids sit by it and read
During their spares
And stay after school

Or come early
To make sure
No one wipes you away.

The principal made an announcement
Saying anyone caught writing on
Or skipping class to guard the wall

Will get detention
But they are calling it
"The Freedom Wall"

There's even a Facebook page!
I think the janitor whatshisname
Is on your side

He has refused to clean it off
Anyway, people are using
Permanent ink

They would have to paint
To cover it up
Someone drew a kind of frame

All Celtic swirls and thorns
It's amazing
I wish you could see it

I'll send you a picture
Or check Facebook
They update the image daily

It's so cool, habibti
You're famous
I'm proud to be your boyfriend

It's like you awoke something
Like everyone at this school
Suddenly gets it.

FAMILY MEETING

When four minds meet
Like four envoys
Each from a faraway land
At first we cannot communicate

We speak different languages
And have different customs
And different beliefs
And want different things

But slowly we begin to understand
Each other, to sympathize
And even agree
On some simple ideas

We eat together, break bread
And share wine
And eventually laugh
About our shared problems

There are "non-negotiables"
Homework and curfews
And sacrifices
Church and clothes

And we all agree
Mom should have therapy
And Kayli, a tutor
And I need to stay out of jail.

DAD: PART TWO

He's just about to adjourn the meeting
I'm expecting Mom to say something
Or Kayli even, but they are silent
I guess they're leaving it up to me
Like I have all the credibility right now.

Dad, I say, you have a place in all this
He turns to me, an open face
Like a window to an empty attic room
With space to pack with broken furniture
And other unwanted things.

We need you around
We need to know that you care
About us as much as you care
About your students
We're your family.

We need you to face up to stuff
Mom has an eating disorder
Kayli has a learning problem
I don't know what's wrong with me
Maybe I'm just attention seeking.

But it's you we all need
Not doctors
Or tutors
Or lawyers
You.

HOMESCHOOLING

By noon Kayli has mastered Pythagoras
And is using his theorem to design a quilt.

When Dad comes home at three
They apply said theorem to a wall bracket.

Next Kayli announces confidently
She's going to build a doghouse.

Maybe start with a birdhouse, Dad says
You're allergic to dogs.

WORD

By email first
Then two texts
Then the Freedom Wall
Facebook page
Posts a photo
Word gets to me

Puffy's lavender watercolor
Has been defaced
The words *JEW* and *KIKE*
Scrawled in black paint
Dripping like vile blood
A vampire's tag.

And beneath
In smaller letters
More words, smaller words
Looping across the soft pastels
In black permanent marker
I feel myself choke
As the picture uploads
    Free Palestine
It reads.

MYSTERY

No one seems to know

How
Or
When

It happened
But this morning when Sarah arrived
To stand guard at the Freedom Wall
The damage was done

No one is sure

Who
Or
Why

But Freckle texts me:

Thrs nly 1 plstnian at schl
Cn u tlk 2 Smr?

TRUST

But before I get the chance, he calls
Meet me at Starbucks, he says

I haven't left the house in four days
But I agree, and change out of my pajamas

Cinnamon-scented steam rises
From the cups on the table between us.

Everyone thinks I did it, don't they?
Freckle, I mean Genie thinks so, I admit

Something about saying her real name
Troubles me, I don't know why.

Freckle? Samir says, with a smile
You're hilarious. That suits her so well.

We sip our chai, holding hands
Did you do it? I finally ask.

Samir looks into my eyes
I feel myself catch fire, burn to ashes

And blow away on a gust of wind
As someone opens the door.

No, I quickly say, Samir lets go
Of my hand and says, *No, I didn't. No.*

FATHERING

With eagle eye
Now that we have told him
We rely
On his strength
Dad's vision and concern
Will go to any length.

Kayli tells me you're upset
Dad says later
What he doesn't get
Would fill a lake
But I tell him anyway
For his sake:

Why do I have to mistrust
So universally
Can't I just
Love Samir and believe
He tells the truth?
Is that naïve?

Because deep down I feel
Some doubt
Small doubt, but solid and real
He used that black paint
In his art, which I guess
Is why I feel so faint.

Dad nods, looking wise
And tells me
Love can cloud our eyes
And those in love are easily misled
Sometimes you should ignore your heart
And listen to your head.

AND ANOTHER THING

Two in the morning
Staring at the dark ceiling
My phone beeps
On the desk

Hala dlvrd boy. V prmture.
Pray. Luv Samir.

Oh God, dear God, I start
But can't go on
Because why should I ask for help
From someone whose fault it is?

Sndng luv. R U at hosp?
Im awke. Call?

Then I wait, wondering
How I can confess I haven't prayed
And hoping maybe he won't ask
My phone rings.

Why are you up so late?
Or did my text wake you?

I was awake, couldn't sleep
Just thinking about everything
Are you okay?
Have you seen the baby?

Just through a window here in NICU
He's tiny and red. Poor angel.

I bite back tears
Thinking of Gabriel.
He'll make it, I'm sure, I say
They can do amazing things now.

The doctors say it's no one's fault
But Hala blames herself.

Privately I think of God
Mercilessly, capriciously deciding
Who lives and who dies
And when and how.

But she did everything she could
Vitamins, eating right, resting

Do you want to come over
I mean, just to sleep?
I've said it without thinking
And hope, kind of, that he'll say no.

No thanks. Tempting, but I can't
My parents are leaving in a few minutes

He hangs up.
Does it matter, I wonder,
If he defaced Puffy's painting?
Can I live with that?

gdnght thx 4 tlkng 2 me
try 2 sleep luv u

But if he did and he lied
What does that mean?
He wants me to trust him
Does he trust me?

LOGIC

I could pray
For God to let Hala's baby live
And if He did
I might hate Him all the more
For making Samir's family suffer
Needlessly.

Had I some disease
And God cured me
I might ask why
He gave me the disease
In the first place
Does suffering amuse Him?

Mom prays for strength
To resist her compulsions
And she claims she finds it
But why would God
Make such a defective brain
That can go so horribly wrong?

I know Mom and Dad both pray
When Kayli gasps for breath
Once her lips turned blue
While we waited for the ambulance
Mom started saying the Hail Mary
And Dad the Lord's Prayer

And the ambulance came
And saved her
Just in time, Mom said
God cleared the traffic
And put the wind at their backs
But why give her asthma at all?

CONFRONTATION

God

Where were you when Gabriel died?

Where were you

When they bulldozed Samir's home

Or when his cousin died?

When buses blow up

When bridges collapse

When little children starve

Or drown

Get shot

Or raped

Do you watch

Or look away?

MY SECRET

Then like an old friend
I recognize the bleak fact
That there is no God.

All those years I was
Talking to myself, praying
To an empty sky.

chapter thirteen

CHIFFON

AND NOW SAMIR

In the middle of Mom's history lesson
(Which, frankly, is quite bizarre)
The doorbell rings

Samir, red-faced, from running
And cold
And…

They sent me home from school
"Pending investigation"
David's father is on the warpath again

"Hate crime" they are calling it
I wish I HAD done it
They don't know what a hate crime is.

He has tears in his eyes
I know he didn't do it
How could I have ever thought he would?

Despite Mom's disapproval
I drag him upstairs, and hold him
Until he stops trembling.

RACHEL

I call Puffy's mother
It's all I can think to do.
We meet at the falafel place
Because Samir has a shift at Starbucks.

I love baklava, she says
Licking honey from her fingers
You look better
How is your mom?

Samir didn't do it, I say
She looks doubtful, then sighs
We left Israel to get away from all that
But it has followed us here.

Samir respects art; that's not his way.
His painting was very hurtful to us
To him too, I say
That's why he painted it.

If he didn't do it, who did?
I don't know, I confess
Sarah is very upset, so is Genie
And when she says Genie

Genie, I remember the name
Genie, swirled onto my math book

The numbers too, but the name
The last *e* in Genie, looped and sideways

Just like the last *e* in *Free Palestine.*

GENI-EEEEEE

I have to go now
(My coffee is about to come back up)
I have to go now
(This horror is about to get worse)
I have to go now
(I have to think of a way to prove it)
I have to go now
(Genie did it; that's so messed up)
I have to go now
(Why would she do it to her own best friend?)
I have to go now
(Even I don't get the psychology here)
I have to go now
(I thought Genie and I were becoming friends)
I have to go now
Thank you, Rachel, for your help
On Christmas Day
And your understanding now
But I have to go.

REHEARSAL

The anti-virus I installed was a free trial
It just expired.
They say there's a nasty worm going around
Let me update you to the full version
And run a scan on Pinky.
It will take a couple of hours
Maybe overnight might be best
Do you want to just leave it here?
I'll come by later to get it.

Then I pick up the phone
And dial.

PINKY

Pinky sits expectant
Like she understands
My devious plans
As though she invites my hands
To tear apart her files
She smiles
Her musical greeting
As if we're meeting
For the first time
But this is the second crime
I've inflicted on poor Pinky.

Pinky opens up
Like a flower in the sun
Ready to be pollinated
Or invaded, investigated.
This would be so fun
If it wasn't for the dumb reason
I'm committing this act of treason
On someone I thought I knew
While admitting
I don't want it to be true
But Pinky doesn't care.

Laid bare
Like a corpse on a slab
In some damp and spooky
Underground lab

While some freaky Dr. Frankenstein
That's me
Pokes around the guts
To see what I can see
And finds enough useless stuff
To write a cheesy girl book
But Pinky's not off the hook

Yet.
I will never forget the feeling
Like it's someone's heart
I'm stealing back,
Because I thought it was mine
But all the time
There was a piece, a slice
A serving of a smile
That maybe I was undeserving
I find a file, which I unlock
In shock and fear
A file named
Samir.

EXCERPTS FROM GENIE'S JOURNAL: LAST YEAR

We held hands on the bus
Samir has the softest hands...

...He kissed me in the hallway
By the gym
No one saw
My lips are still tingling...

...No one can know
Especially not Dad.
I can't even tell Sarah.
She would be horrified...

...Samir has this new friend, Khalid
He's an über-Muslim
All praying and fasting and long sleeves
The whole fundy package...

...We were going to do it!
But Samir didn't show up tonight
When Dad came home at one thirty
I had to tell him I watched a sad movie
Because he could tell I'd been crying...

...Samir wouldn't talk to me today at school
He said he had to rush to math

But there was at least five minutes
Until the bell...

...I'll never forgive him
How could he do this?
We were so in love.

AND FINALLY

A Facebook message
From Sarah to Genie
U don't really think Sam did it do u?
And Genie's reply
Who cares?
Even Sarah is shocked.
How can u say that?
That's so cold.
He could go to jail!
But Genie is unmoved
He and LA will have that in common.

But privately
In a file it takes forty-five minutes to hack into
Genie writes:

I'm so scared.
I don't know what to do.
What if they DO arrest him?
Or if Sarah finds out?
She'll disown me
For writing those words
I'm such an idiot
Samir just used me
But I still love him
I've got no one to talk to
I wish Mom was here
I wish I was dead.

GRATITUDE

Mom is writing in her gratitude journal
It's something her therapist recommends
When I sit down beside her she shows me
The top of each page reads *my girls*

Then the words *three minutes*
She always says, when she can talk about it
That she's grateful little Gabriel
Wasn't born dead.

Every page, every day, starts the same way:
My girls and *three minutes.*
He knew his mother, she says, *heard my voice*
He opened his eyes and looked at me

And you two, you're like the two sides
The two ventricles of my heart.
Me, I'm awash with gratitude right now
That the medication is right

The mood is under control
The vomiting has stopped
Because right now, more than anything
I need my mom.

I tell her everything, every little detail
Samir, the condoms even, Genie, the "hate crime"

The unlocked file, the awful truth
And all the while she holds my hand.

And when I finish she knows just what to say
So we have your side, you seem to know
The other girl's side too, her story
Now it is time to talk to this boy.

WHEN A BOY CRIES IN STARBUCKS

It is powerful
And heartbreaking

It is unexpected
Yet vindicating

He is contrite
And begs forgiveness

I wanted to tell you
But I promised her

She was so angry at me
And didn't want anyone to know

It wasn't serious
We were just kids

It was only last year, I say
Have you grown up so much?

We didn't do anything
Just kissed a couple of times

She seems to think you planned
To go all the way

She wanted to; I didn't
I was very confused last year

You're still confused aren't you?
No, not about you; I love you.

BUT FIRST, MY LAWYER CALLS

What a joke our justice system is
When charges are traded
Like baseball cards
I'll give you misdemeanor, suspended
If you give me hate crime.

Hate crime, it seems, is valuable
It gets media, it gets cred
Whereas pinning a sex crime
On a sixteen-year-old girl
Is starting to lose its gloss

They think I know something
And are willing to deal for information
My Lawyer thinks public opinion
Has turned in my favor
But David's father will be disappointed

If he had only asked two hours ago
I would have happily turned them both in
And let God sort them out
But boy tears and reflection
Changed my mind.

There is no anti-Semite thug
Just a mixed-up girl
Who one hour ago I might have hated
But now I pity
I know how it feels to love Samir.

HONESTY

After all,
Who am I to judge?
Neither of us realized
What we did
Was considered criminal

After all
She and I
Are not so different
That's just the sort of stupid thing
I would do

After all
We both love the same boy
But he only loves one of us back
I think; he could have used us both
After all.

SORRY GENIE

Sorry Genie
But I know it was you
I recognized the way you write your *e*
I read your journal
And made copies of the files

Sorry Genie
It's best if you don't make a scene
I'm telling you before anyone else
Except Samir, he knows
But I think he suspected all along

Sorry Genie
I lied to you about your laptop
I needed to find out the truth
Because I knew Samir was innocent
You understand

Sorry Genie
If we hurt you
I didn't know you were ever with him
He kept your secret like you asked
That's got to be worth something

Sorry Genie
But we're both so deeply in trouble
If someone asks, and they will
If I know who wrote those words
I have to tell them.

THE LOOK ON HER FACE

Could launch a thousand ships
Could cleave your heart in twain
Could make a grown man cry
Could raise the dead

But nothing could prepare me
For her reaction.

When hell freezes over…
To the ends of the earth…
Until the day I die…

And something about the end of the universe.

THE OFFICE

Volatile
The three of us
(Because Samir witnessed the whole sorry scene)
Are sitting in the office
The principal wants our stories
And, of course, Genie goes first

Confident
Samir takes my hand and whispers
This is going to end badly
Then we kiss, tenderly
Until the secretary clears her throat
Samir puts his arm around my shoulders

Defiant
I imagine noosing Genie
And pulling the knot tight
Because I know what she's doing
How she is twisting the truth
To suit her situation

Impassive
The principal emerges
And speaks in clipped tones
To the shocked secretary
Please ask security to escort these two out
Behind him, Genie stares

Triumphant.

ODE TO LAWYERS

When you have a lawyer

You can skip the nasty parts
Like being arrested
For stealing a laptop

They can phone you
When you're on the bus
And break the bad news

They can explain the new charges
Without sounding impatient
That you've screwed up again

You can say things like
I didn't steal it, she gave it to me
And leave out the part about tricking her

And when you say
What if I just leave town?
They can't tell your parents

They pretend to be on your side
And charge $250 per hour
To listen to you sob with frustration.

You have someone who knows everything
And who will maybe understand
When you decide to run away.

SAMIR'S BROTHER

My love
Have I told you about my brother?
My father likes to pretend
He doesn't exist

My brother
Is older than Hala
By three years
Ten years older than me

My brother
Remembers the shelling
The house being torn down
Things I can't remember at all

My brother
Didn't want to marry
The girl my parents suggested
He didn't want to marry any girl

My brother
Lives in New York
I think he will take us in
If you don't mind that he's gay

My God
Of course you don't mind
You are the only one
Who accepts everyone as they are.

PACKING

It feels like only days ago
I packed this stuff
I'll start again
I told myself
I'll start
Again

                                          Again
                                     I'll start
                              A packed bag
                         A promise to try
                   To stay out of trouble

Two train tickets east   A train ticket east
And a declaration
Of true love
A dream
Escape
Us

                                           We
                                     Need
                                Each other
                           A few clothes
                      Long-sleeved shirts

A pink dress   A vintage dress I wore once
Appears, resurrected
I threw it away
And yet
There
It is

It is
The dress
I tried to leave
Like the part of me
That refuses to conform
I hope they like it in New York.

THE PINK CHIFFON DRESS

Mom thought it was from the '60s,
Maybe the '70s
I found it at the thrift store
By the soup kitchen
I liked how soft the fabric was
Like waves of pink cobwebs

And I liked that it had long sleeves
And a high neck
Because I hated to show too much
I loved the bright color
And the way it moved
When I twirled in the fitting room

I liked how bold it seemed
At the black and white ball
The girls in their little black sheaths
All collarbones and pushed-up boobs
And me a fluffy little pink flower
Glowing in the slag pile

Though I don't remember dancing in it
And there are no pictures of me at the dance
Just an elusive memory of some excitement
Some kind of scene that Mom and Dad
Were not happy about (what's new?)
And nausea because I got so drunk.

It's a little loose now
I've lost some shape
From stress, maybe
But it still makes me feel powerful
Feminine, strong, safe and
Like myself again.

KAYLI

Nice dress, says Kayli
I think it's possessed, I say
It followed me from the old house

Kayli laughs
I rescued it from the charity pile
It's so you, you can't give it away

I'm going to wear it every day
I say, until I graduate
That might be forever

I have come down to the pink-palace boudoir
To deliver a gift
One of the *A*'s from *Audacious*

The "asthmatic" Kayli looks sunken
And scared, breathless
Just like our imagined doomed heroines

I'm not sure what audacious means
She says, as we hang up the canvas
I mean I don't think I am anyway

Her walls are the same shade of pink
As the floaty vintage dress
I could disappear in here, I joke

But Kayli doesn't laugh
I know you want to disappear, she says
I hid that dress in a suitcase

And why would you open a suitcase
If you weren't planning on using it?
To that I have no answer.

chapter fourteen

THE SEND-OFF

No one wants to hear this:
Is that what you're wearing?
Mom says it, eyeing my pink chiffon
Wouldn't something black…?
Would The Phantom wear black to a funeral?
I ask, even her own?

But Mom frowns silently all the way to church
It took her this long to find some family
And bus them in from the south.
The Phantom's brother is a veteran
He used to visit her, send her money
But then he had a stroke and things got tight.

He limps up the aisle and stands
By the plain coffin the church paid for
His wife sits pinch-lipped and silent
Like poor Charlotte couldn't even die right
The photo on the casket looks nothing like her
But I have a remedy for that.

Ugly, it reads, unashamedly
She was what she was
Vulgar, rude, crazy, drunk
Puzzle pieces loosely fitting together
She was a question, the answer to which
Only she knew.

Afterward Mom talks to the brother
Consoles him, poor man
He did all he could
She was never the same, he says
After her son died in the accident
And Mom cries and cries, later in the car.

NINA

She finds it
Driving through snow and tears
The house over the train tracks
It is still festooned with Christmas lights
And Santa's face grins on the door
Nice dress, Nina says to me
Jiggling her son on her hip
And invites us in
Mom gazes longingly at the baby
And Nina obliges.

Nina loves her canvas: *Indigenous*
I look smart, she says
You are smart, I point out
You think? I was no good at school
Smart people seldom are, I say
I came to the show, you know
That first night
She shakes her head, smiling
Howah, you got some balls
Putting up a picture like that
Then to my mother: *excuse me, ma'am.*

Mom doesn't hear
She's deep in a game
Of competitive peekaboo
And the baby boy seems to be winning
I'm going back to school, Nina says

If I can pass some tests this summer
I'll be in grade twelve with you
I need to find a tutor I can afford
I look over at Mom
I think I know someone, I say.

MAYBE

After I run away
Nina and her baby might
Take my place, with Mom.

This I tell myself
Is how she'll survive my loss
Even forgive me.

COLD

The weather changes
A sharp wind blows from the North
Too cold for just tights,
I slip some skinny jeans
Under the vintage dress
And boots, coat and hat
Stomp through the thick falling snow
To Starbucks.

Nice dress, Samir says
We sit cozy in the big corner chair
He slips his black-and-white scarf
(Keffiyeh, I know this is called)
From around his neck
And carefully wraps it
Over my hair

This is how the cool Muslim girls dress
With pretty long-sleeved dresses
Over sexy jeans
Who are they kidding that this is modest?
You look hot.

Samir kisses me, a first.
He has not kissed me in public
Since that night after the art show
I blush, and tug the scarf down.

I have my dad's car, he whispers
We could leave right now
And be in New York by Friday.
You're going to steal your dad's car?
I ask, incredulous, but intrigued
No, YOU'RE going to steal it, he says
You're the thief, remember?

LOOSE ENDS

But neither of us thinks
It will really happen
This way
We have talked
About taking the train.

We take our mochas to go
And Samir drives me to Ms. Sagal's

Almost wordlessly
I deliver her canvas: *Single*
And Marika's: *Disabled*

She doesn't say much
And when we leave
Samir speculates
I hear she's coming back to school
They probably told her
Not to talk to us.

That stings me
But feels oddly familiar.

I'm like a flower
Whose petals are being plucked away
One by one
Or falling to the ground
Their purpose served.

When I hold the last petal
Samir
I wonder
Will I say, "He loves me"?

BLACK ICE

Driving with Samir
Slowly, around
The outskirts of town
The roads are being plowed
But Samir has been warned
Of Black Ice.

Black ice is invisible
It looks like a clear road
But it tricks you
Next thing you know
You're spinning
Out of control.

Then we're quiet
For a minute
As we absorb that potent
Metaphor.

Samir parks the car
Out near the airport
Even though it's dark,
It's only four thirty
Cold enough
That we can see our breath
Even in the car.
I love you, I say
In a cloud of mist

And touch his face
With my fuzzy glove
He closes his eyes
Takes my hand
And drags me, gently,
Into the backseat.

C-C-C-C-COLD

It's much too cold
To do more than unzip our coats
And lie face to face
Wrapped in each other
For warmth.

I remove one fuzzy glove
And snake my hand
Between us
To the button of his jeans
Don't, he breathes

It's just touching, I say
It won't take much
We'll get all sticky
Anyway, he adds ironically
It's a sin to spill it.

Maybe I could catch it
In a coffee cup, I say
Which makes us both laugh
So hard that he falls off the seat
And onto the floor.

He climbs back up painfully
And pulls me into a deep kiss
I slide into his lap
Joined at the hip
We forget the cold

Until the door opens
And a man's head appears
Who the hell are you?
I say as Samir squirms out from under me
That's my dad, he says.

CAUGHT

Samir drives
His sister sits in the back next to me
A chaperone
While Samir's father drives ahead
In one of the company trucks.

It was the snow that doomed us
A plow driver
Recognized Samir's father's car
And, worried, called his cell phone
I guess he knew what he'd find.

Has he taken your virginity? Hala says
Hala! Samir says
Followed by a string of Arabic
Which his sister returns in kind
Before turning back on me.

Guarding your chastity is a test
But the reward is great
A woman's virginity
Is given to her by God
For her to give to her husband.

Thanks, I say
But I like to think I have other gifts
As for what I have between my legs
That's the gift that keeps on giving
I'll give that to whomever I please.

I can see Samir in the rearview
Trying not to laugh
Sometimes I'm sure
He's as shocked by the things I say
As I am.

SAMIR'S HOUSE

Samir and I sit
At the kitchen table
While Hala makes tea.

I can hear Samir's parents
Talking in Arabic
In the next room

What are they saying?
I ask Samir
He listens for a moment

They're talking about me
And the Muslim School
As if that matters now

Samir's father comes in
And sits across from me
As Samir literally hangs his head.

Is he ashamed of me, I wonder
But his father speaks
Samir told me he loves you, he says

I feel the heat radiating out from my heart
Like a fire, spreading in a dry field
I know I'm blushing but I don't care

Love is a blessing and a gift
His father says, unexpectedly
Not for us to question.

Do you love my son too?
Yes, I say, emphatically
Yes, so much it hurts.

Across from me, Samir sighs.
His eyes, through the prison-bar lashes,
Look up and meet mine

His father continues
Love requires sacrifice
What would you give up for my son?

Anything, I say, without hesitation
Everything. I think
Of Ella, abandoned on the rooftop

Half-formed, ill-thought Ella
Who never had a chance
To blossom

Ella, who was going to change my life
Who was going to be the change
That remade me in her image.

Ella, who would never hack a laptop
Display genitalia
Or fall in love with the wrong boy

Ella and her plan
To blend in, thrive
And avoid controversy

Ella, who I wish had answered
Politely, thoughtfully
Diplomatically

When Samir's father asked
Do you love my son enough
To become a Muslim?

Instead it was me
Raphaelle
Who simply laughed.

RAPHAELLE FAILS THE TEST

My laughter dies in pain and silence
Samir's father says something
But I can't hear him
My heart pounds
in my ears

Because Samir is looking at me
And I can read his eyes
Disappointed
They say
Betrayed.

Then I'm out in the snow
Coat open and cold
Samir follows me
Please don't go
He says

It doesn't matter, he lies
God has joined us
He wants us to
Be together
Forever

Samir, I say, marveling at the snowflakes
Drifting down between us in the dark
And there are so many things
I want to say but all I
Can say is:

Samir, listen to me
I don't believe
In your god
Or any
God.

PURGING: PART TWO

And so much follows
That I almost believe
It is me who incites
A blizzard to blow up.

Snow swirls around us
Like a poltergeist
And Samir's tears
Freeze on his face.

How can there be a god
I cry into the wind
When babies die minutes
After they're born?

How could your god let
Israel take your land?
How could their god
Let six million of them burn?

What kind of god
Would let those things happen?
Does he watch?
Does he laugh and enjoy it?

How could he let your father
Pretend he only has one son?
If being gay is not okay with God
Why does he allow it?

What the fuck does he have planned for me?
Am I supposed to go to jail
Ruin my life over a painting?
Maybe he just wants me to kill myself

Like Van Gogh
Maybe I should just carve off
Some body parts first
Maybe my nose

Or my breasts before
He fills them with cancer
Poke out my eyes
Before he blinds me.

Habibti, don't talk like that
You don't mean it
God loves you
I love you.

God loves me?!
If this is love I dread to see
What God would do
If he hated me.

How could God
Let those girls, those bitches
Lock me in the dark under the stairs
IN THE DARK, I scream, for the whole night?!

Suddenly I feel light-headed and hot
What girls? Samir says
What are you talking about?
For a blissful second I'm not sure

Then something acrid bubbles up inside me
I turn and vomit tea into a snowdrift
And want more than anything else
To tear off the pink dress.

Samir tries to stop me
But I pull away
And run
Home.

FOUR-WHEEL DRIVE: PART TWO

The Range Rover appears
A flash of blue in the whiteout

Dad jumps out and scoops me up
Like a little girl
Like he did once
When one of those cunts finally
Confessed the next day
That I was locked under the stairs
In the old auditorium.

He burst through the door
With police behind him
And wordlessly scooped me up.
I dropped the bottle I'd held all night
Empty, it shattered on the concrete floor
My raincoat smelled of whiskey
And puke

There was an ambulance that time
But this time he buckles me in
Beside him and tucks his own coat
Around me.
Your young man called
He's very upset
What happened?

What happened Dad?
What happened that night
At my junior-high dance?
How did you manage to lose me?
Rah Rah, he says, *you asked us not to come*
You wanted to go alone.
And then you didn't come home.

I can't stop shivering
Dad cranks the heat up
As high as it will go
I didn't think you remembered
Much of that, Dad says
You were so drunk when we found you.
They had to pump your stomach.

That girl saved your life.
She called us when she heard
Told us she saw you around there
And remembered how the door would lock.
I grab Dad's arm and tell him to stop.
Stop talking.

Stop the car.

I'm crying
Like I have never cried in my life
Dad, I say, I didn't go down there alone

Those girls took me down there
Lured me down there
To drink with them
And then locked me in.

Locked me in the dark
In the cold
Nothing but concrete,
Whiskey and me
Mocked me through the door
And left me
To not quite die.

Dad pulls the parking brake
Are you sure?
Now I'm wailing: I'm so messed up
I'm going to go to jail
Or something terrible.
Samir and I were going to run away.
I don't know what to do.

I'm so sorry Daddy, I say
I've screwed up so badly this time
I wanted to be better
I really tried
You didn't do anything wrong, Dad says
My girl, my Rah Rah.
I'll fix it.

chapter fifteen

TRUTH

SOAK

Samir calls, six times
While I'm soaking in the tub
Shivering, and finally
Being dressed by Mom
In flannel pajamas
And put into bed.

I'll speak to the boy, she says
You need to sleep.
The phone stops ringing
I lie in bed, looking at the pink dress
On the floor where I discarded it
And will it to burst into flames

Of course it doesn't
Because there are no such things
As miracles.

As for sleep
That's not likely
My head is ringing

Their voices
What they shouted
Through the locked door
As I begged them
To let me out
Of the dark
That word they called me
It started with C.

RECKONING

It was a bad year, says Mom
Although I pretend to be asleep
She knows better.

I should have noticed
I should have been available for you
But I was trapped in my own grief
For Nana
And for Gabriel.

Now this year
I've done it again
Caught up in my own bullshit.

At this, I turn and look at her
Mom never swears in front of me.

I can do something for you
I know this boy, Samir
He didn't deface that painting
I know you know who did
Why don't you tell someone?

So I do
And half an hour later
I'm dressed
Sitting at the dining room table
Across from Genie
And her dad.

GENIE'S LAST STAND

She denies everything
And claims I faked my evidence
Her journal entries
And her loopy handwriting
Mean nothing to her.

I can see her father
Losing patience
And I get the feeling
This is not the first time
Genie has been caught in a lie.

But we get nowhere
She refuses to confess
And I adamantly defend Samir
And our long-suffering parents
Sigh and press their lips together.

Finally I ask to speak to Genie alone
I don't have time for this, I say
I'm going to court tomorrow
For something I know I did do
I might end up in jail

So let's get this out in the open
You have a score to settle with Samir?
Here, talk to him
I dial and hand her my phone
And then I go back to bed.

FACEBOOK PRIVATE MESSAGES

From Genie

I told sarah. she called david's dad and told him. he's dropping the case. happy? i've lost my bff thanks to u. u and samir deserve each other.
if u tell anyone else i'll kill u. BTW i've changed ALL my passwords.
-g
UNFRIEND

To Samir

How did you get her to change her mind about telling the truth?
-r

From Samir

Don't be mad, but you're not the only one who's taken a naked picture. Good thing I saved the ones she sent to me.
I love you
-sam

To Samir

You saved them? Why did you save them?
-r

From Samir

Is there any answer that will make me NOT seem like a total dick?
Still love you
-sam

REASON

There is some reason left in the world
Apparently
The judge rules that my art is just that.
Art, she says
Must be taken in context.

Since I was not the one
Who sent the image as a text
And when she is about to reveal
Who actually did
David's father objects!
The judge glares at him but says
Sustained

What a seriously screwed-up system.
As for the "hate crime"
The laptop and Freckle
None of that is mentioned.

I leave the courthouse
Not a criminal
Not a sex offender
Just me
A misfit troublemaker
In mismatched shoes.

I HATE HOSPITALS

The smell, I think
Disinfectant on vinyl
Latex and bleach
And mashed potatoes

In neonatal
All of this is covered
With a cloud of baby poo
Spit-up, anxiety and grief

Hala watches her tiny son
Through the incubator plastic
Her hand resting beside him
His spidery fingers around her thumb.

I leave her *Arab* canvas, wrapped
And look for Mom to leave
But she's sitting next to Hala
Samir appears in the doorway

What is his name?
Mom asks, and Hala clears her throat
Jibreel, it is an angel's name
The same as the English Gabriel

Mom catches her breath
And takes Hala's other hand
A moment passes so full
I think I hear the walls creak

Expanding to fit
The weight of heartbreak and hope
Samir and I lock eyes, knowing
We have just witnessed a miracle, of sorts.

THE END

Are you coming back to school?

Do you want me to?

I don't know…my…

You're breaking up with me, aren't you?

I'm so sorry
I still love you

What difference does that make?

It should make a difference
But I don't think I can be with you
Without becoming someone else.
Someone who I don't want to be
Who I can't be
And still be me.

Innocent and free. No parents, no school
No religion
No you, no me.

I meant those things when I said them
But things have changed

They haven't changed for me
I love YOU
Not what you believe

I am what I believe
Because I believe
Jibreel is going to live, Inshā Allāh

I know what that means
"If God wills it"
If that is who your god is
I don't like Him.

You don't understand

No, I don't.
We're too different.
I'm an adult
And you are a child.

MEMORY

That stung him
And the memory of his face
His pain
Sustains me.

Later
The memory of his hands
And lips and tongue
Derails me.

The pink dress hangs
In a dry-cleaning bag
In my closet
I lay it on the bed

Can I have it?
Kayli says behind me.
I want to wear it to Spring Fling
I narrow my eyes.

You? I say
Don't you prefer something
More revealing?
Kayli blushes prettily.

A boy asked me to go, but he
Wants me to wear something…
I groan. Modest? I say
He's not…

A Mormon, Kayli says
And we both laugh until
Dad calls up the stairs
Telling us to turn off the gas.

WITHOUT HIM

But later
My laughter turns
To tears

I cry and cry
Samir's last words to me
You don't understand

Cut, deep an untruth
An accusation
I cannot bear

I understand everything
What it's like
How empty

How pointless
Heartless
And perplexing

To live
Without
Him.

TINY

The photograph
Lovingly framed
Then wrapped in blue tissue
And tied with white satin

I don't look at it much anymore, Mom says
Maybe I should.
She peels back the ribbon
The paper falls away

It is a tiny photo, black and white
Two impossibly small feet
He weighed less than a pound, she says
Like a sprite, he could have curled up in my hand

Darling Gabriel,
Whose only task on earth
Was to break my mother's heart.
It took him his whole life.

Can you make a painting?
Her uncertainty is unbearable
Because I would move planets
And eat snakes for her, for Gabriel.

CHALLENGE

Samir's father's words
Rattle around my head
Love is a blessing and a gift
Not for us to question.

But

Of love
I have so many questions
It would take to the end of the universe
To ask them all.

LEARNER'S LICENSE

I need a canvas
A big one
And Dad has taken the car.

My fingers ache to call Samir
I know he loves the art-supply place
But somehow, it's David I dial.

He arrives, driving, his brother beside him
I got my learner's license, he says with glee.
His brother is so painfully gorgeous

That my words get tangled as I say hello
I sit in the back, contemplating
How David and his brother look very alike.

I'm glad you called, David says
I'm so sorry about all the…that was NOT cool.
Beside him, his brother whistles.

I'm grounded beyond Pluto
But this is "homework" so we can hang out.
Michael will wait in the car, right?

Michael grunts and pulls out an iPhone
I stroll with David, looking at paint
And marveling at my capriciousness.

I heard you broke up with Sam, David says
God, I say, is someone blogging my life?
Genie told me, he says, *she's moving in for the kill.*

It's so funny I nearly laugh
That at the same time I want to murder Genie
I want to kiss David.

NOT FOR US TO QUESTION

Quaint, the idea that love is
Unquestionable undefeatable
Endless fathomless
Strong as time and
Tenacious as space but
If love is never to be tested
Or challenged then it is worth
Nothing.

AUDACIOUS ANGEL

Because you believed
In yourself
Your tiny self

Because you knew
There is no greater accomplishment
Than making someone love you

You only needed three minutes
Your footprints
Like your memory

Larger than life
Larger than you
Or me.

FREEDOM WALL

Time passes,
Like music floating though an open window
And spring arrives.

Mental clarity returns to me piece by piece
And I think I've said all I can say
To my poor shrink.

I'm going back to school after the break
I stop by to pick up some things
David skips, and meets me by the wall.

We have been "hanging out"
Since he has returned from Pluto
And once, he kissed me.

He's not my boyfriend
I think even he senses Samir
Lingering in the corners of my heart.

I've even apologized
He says he doesn't mind
But by my wall, he takes my hand

Territorially
I'm glad they left this up
He says of the Freedom Wall

All the other art
David's, Samir's and of course
Sarah's have been taken down.

But the Freedom Wall remains
This is the first time I have seen it
In real life.

I can barely take it in
I'm overwhelmed by the honesty
And simplicity of the sentiments

I decide, someone has written
And *He made us ALL perfect,* writes another
And then I see it.

Small and tucked in a corner
A scrawl of Arabic
That I recognize

I googled it once, before Christmas
Thinking I might write it on a card
أنا أحبك

I practiced it about a hundred times
But gave up and went with English.
I know it says: *I love you*

Beside me, David sighs
Impatient, and lets go of my hand
'Sup, Sam? he says

Samir doesn't answer
He gazes in his unraveling way
And David kisses my ear and leaves.

Are you two…?
Just friends, I say, not that you should care.
My heart is pounding.

How is Jibreel? I say to change the subject
He weighs six pounds
Like he was born yesterday

But beautiful, so beautiful
Like his uncle, I think
And Samir says, *I miss you.*

TRUTH

I could miss him too
But my ear remembers David's kiss
David is in Students for Secular Humanism
And Samir in the Islamic Students' Alliance.

I could have David as a "boyfriend"
Tolerate his low-slung jeans
And his hockey friends thinking they know me
Because they've seen a picture of my snatch.

I could make love with Samir
Right now, baptize him inside me
Spirit him back to the mudroom door
And take him on the narrow stairs.

I could walk away
From both of them
From another school, another crisis
I could walk away from myself.

Be Ella again, finally
Measured and careful
Popular and successful
Ella would choose

But Raphaelle
Wants what she wants

She can't think of a reason not
To have her baklava.

And eat it too.

THE QUESTION

So just because I can
I'm going to have two boyfriends

One for Ella: the popular rich boy
Hockey jock with an artistic streak

One for Raphaelle: the moody, pious Muslim
Handsome and hot-blooded with a body to match

One for movies and parties
One for furtive tumbles and soul-searching

One for my head
And one for my heart

I will try to keep them from each other
I don't want anyone to get hurt

Although both of them hurt me
I'm done with vengeance

I know it's capricious, maybe selfish
But in the end that could be

                    the
                        whole
                            truth
                                about
                                    me.

ACKNOWLEDGMENTS

It started with Sonya Sones, who introduced me to the idea of a verse novel for teens and got me addicted to the form. Ellen Hopkins was and continues to be an inspiration and cheerleader for novels in verse and verse novelists.

Carrie Gleason read this manuscript first and sent me a soul-nourishing email that I read over a bowl of Vietnamese noodles. Kris Rothstein and Carolyn Swayze listened to my big wish for this book, then made it come true. Sarah Harvey and Andrew Wooldridge weren't at all fazed by the four-letter word at the heart of this story.

My sister, Monica Prendergast, a poet and scholar, gave me a confidence-building reality check when it all started to seem a little scary. My other sisters, Tess and Kathy, just believe in me, no questions asked. Mum's perplexity about my love of young-adult literature makes me laugh. Dad, wherever you are, I know you noticed, eventually.

My husband, Len, and daughter, Lucy, tolerate my moods, poor housekeeping and general nonsense.

To all of you, thanks.

GABRIELLE PRENDERGAST

is a UK-born Canadian/Australian who lives in Vancouver, BC, with her husband and daughter. She holds an MFA in Creative Writing from the University of British Columbia. A part-time teacher and mentor, Gabrielle blogs and rants at Angelhorn.com and VerseNovels.com.

Ella's
story
continues...

CAPRICIOUS

coming soon...

ORCA BOOK PUBLISHERS
www.orcabook.com • 1-800-210-5277